WILLIAM MORRIS

Stories from Potowasso

Morality Tales from a Small Town

iUniverse, Inc.
Bloomington

Copyright © 2011 by William Morris

All rights reserved. No part of this book may be used or reproduced by any means, graphic, electronic, or mechanical, including photocopying, recording, taping or by any information storage retrieval system without the written permission of the publisher except in the case of brief quotations embodied in critical articles and reviews.

iUniverse books may be ordered through booksellers or by contacting:

iUniverse
1663 Liberty Drive
Bloomington, IN 47403
www.iuniverse.com
1-800-Authors (1-800-288-4677)

Because of the dynamic nature of the Internet, any web addresses or links contained in this book may have changed since publication and may no longer be valid. The views expressed in this work are solely those of the author and do not necessarily reflect the views of the publisher, and the publisher hereby disclaims any responsibility for them.

Any people depicted in stock imagery provided by Thinkstock are models, and such images are being used for illustrative purposes only.

Certain stock imagery © Thinkstock.

ISBN: 978-1-4502-9642-7 (sc)
ISBN: 978-1-4502-9641-0 (hc)
ISBN: 978-1-4502-9640-3 (ebook)

Library of Congress Control Number: 2011902321

Printed in the United States of America

iUniverse rev. date: 03/15/2011

To Susan, who makes life rich.

Contents

Introduction	ix
A Christmas Blessing	1
The Christmas Program	9
Christmas on Sunday	19
Christmas Blackout	33
A New Year's Resolution	43
Irish Green	57
Spring Break	65
Gourmet Hash	73
The Sunday Budget Meeting	81
The Music School of Hard Knocks	89
The Big Scoop	101
A Sweet-and-Sour Thanksgiving	113
Hunting Season	123
Hill Folk, Flatlanders, and Table Settings	133

Introduction

Potowasso stories are a compilation of my memories of the small town in which I grew up and the people and places that helped mold me and taught me some basic lessons in life. Most characters are exaggerated a bit or are simple amalgamations of personalities and mannerisms. I call them morality tales because, as I look back, my parents and the larger family—the church and the whole community—were trying to impress me with certain standards of conduct and tutor me in the virtues of being a good person.

When I began to write these stories, I intended to use them in a special Christmas or Advent service instead of my usual Sunday night conventional worship service. I wanted something relaxed, where I simply talked to the folks and then read a story I had written. I asked a friend who played guitar and sang folk and country music to perform at the service. We set a small stage area with an old quilt for a background, a small table with a kerosene lamp, and a rocking chair in which I would sit as I told the story. It went well, and I had demands to do it every year and maybe on some other special occasions also.

I did three Christmas stories on three successive years, which explains why I have written more Christmas stories than other holiday stories, though my range would expand. We began to use more and more music, some extra skits, and even a couple of humorous interviews with church members or guests.

Then I took a call to minister in Northern Michigan and did a Christmas story that first year, and again it was well received. We decided to try to do a monthly program on a Saturday night, and did so calling it "Second Saturday at Moddersville," the Reformed church where I pastored. This meant I would write new stories for different months, trying to use a holiday as a focus for each one.

This church in Northern Michigan and the community in which it served was rural and really down-to-earth. They also had a great love for music, and we began utilizing local musicians and eventually went further and further to find good country, folk, or bluegrass bands to play.

In my fourth year in Northern Michigan, and about eight years since the first Potowasso story was written, my wife, Susan, and I moved to upstate New York to a church in Clarksville, in the hills above Albany. I used the stories I had written on occasion, but we never did regular programs since that move. I guess it was time to go in another writing direction.

As I began writing other projects, I was haunted by the stories set in my fictional town of Potowasso and felt the need to put some of them together and have them published as a way to make a formal break from those stories, as I attempted to go to new things. I also felt that the stories, at least for me, were inseparable from the various settings, musicians, friends, and parishioners that were a part of those special years, and I wanted to honor those memories and give all who were a part of it a keepsake for all those story and music moments.

The first Potowasso story written was "A Christmas Blessing." It's not only the original story, but it is more tenderhearted and less comical than the later ones. As I found my voice in writing these stories, I found more humor in the characters and situations.

The Potowasso stories are set in a range of times, from the late 1950s through the 1990s. From a *Leave It to Beaver* family, to a teen experiencing the Beatles and the first signs of nonconformity, to early experiences as an adult with a family, times changed but the basic lessons seem to always be there if you're willing to look and, most importantly, willing to laugh.

A Christmas Blessing

It was years ago, during a winter where snow and ice would alter the course of tradition and faith. Horace Blessing had been making and delivering fruit-and-nut surprise loaves for almost four decades. But this year it was doubtful; Horace found himself on injured reserve.

Horace sat in the kitchen, absently rubbing his coffee mug with his good hand, the one not limited by the cast that followed his fall on the ice a week ago. "This is the worst time it could happen!" he yelled at the cupboards of the empty kitchen. Then in frustration—a frustration deeper than he had ever remembered—he slammed his fist down on the table, causing coffee to jump from the half-full mug onto the flower oilcloth table covering.

He grabbed the dishrag and wiped up the spilled coffee, thinking that a broken arm was never convenient, but this was a special time for him. It was thirty-seven years that he had been making and delivering the surprise loaf during the week before Christmas.

Rinsing the rag at the sink, he remembered where it had begun. Dalia, his wife, had originated the tradition. She had created the holiday treat the first year they were married. Back then, his only job was to hold his finger on the half-knotted red and green ribbons Dalia tied around the wax paper-covered loaves. They would talk of unimportant things as they worked around the table together. Horace still talked to his bride in the kitchen as he took over all the duties that they once shared.

She died only eight years after they were married. That first Christmas after Dalia's passing, Horace decided to keep Dalia's holiday tradition alive. And in a way, it kept Dalia alive. He would smell the ingredients, and it smelled like Dalia in the kitchen.

Beyond being a labor of love, the fruit-and-nut surprise loaf was an excursion of wishful thinking, or even a bit of denial. And so, the thin layer of ice that precipitated his fall and broke his arm was also a great threat to this most sacred tradition that kept the last part of Dalia alive.

Horace just couldn't let this tradition die. Too much was at stake. It would be like letting Dalia die again. His eyes drifted around the warm kitchen, willing a solution, when he glanced at a Christmas card displayed on the chipped enamel sideboard near the back door and thought to himself, *That's it!*

It was a card from the McIntry family. In that card he perceived a way to get another right hand—a helper. Horace knew just who he would get. Maggie, the fourteen-year-old daughter who was the closest thing to a granddaughter he had—not by blood, but by history with her grandfolks, John and Hazel McIntry.

When Dalia died, John and Hazel displayed more than tears; they revealed a real compassion at his most difficult time. They asked Horace to come and live with them on the farm. They said they needed the help anyway, and Horace was in such a state as to believe them.

The McIntrys converted the old woodshed off the back of the house and made a "hired-hand" room. Horace had breakfast and supper with his hosts but packed a simple lunch and ate outside in good weather and in the barn in bad. He did this out of respect for John and Hazel's need for time alone. The arrangement wasn't perfect, but it was the best he could do for a long time, until he saved up enough money to purchase the old Anderson place in the village limits of Potowasso.

Maggie approached the white two-story house with the white barn out back, peeling to gray. Mr. Blessing had invited her to help him with the fruit-and-nut surprise loaves that were a long-standing tradition. She was happy, honored, and eager to help with this holiday ritual that was such a part of the Potowasso holiday routine, and she quickly agreed.

She understood that she would help him shop for the ingredients, assist in making the famous loaves, and even accompany him to deliver the treats. Maggie was well aware of how much the locals anticipated this annual holiday visit.

Early on this Saturday morning, just a little more than a week before Christmas, she had walked over to Mr. Blessing's house on Gower Street. As she approached, she could see Mr. Blessing step out onto the back porch wearing his red-and-black large-checked wool coat, brown wool pants, black zip-up boots, green cap with earflaps, and bulky black mittens. Mr. Blessing met her at the end of the walkway. He was as she remembered: the stodgy old man with smudged wire-rimmed glasses and a scruffy four-day beard—mostly gray but partially stained with his chewing tobacco dribble.

"Hi, Mr. Blessing," Maggie began.

He avoided further niceties with an abrupt "Let's get to the store."

They went immediately to Gleeder's Market to shop for the necessities for the surprise loaf. Horace and Maggie returned to the house excited about the project. As Maggie unpacked the bags, she examined this old friend of the family while he scrutinized the aged and yellowed recipe card in Dalia's careful script. He sat at the kitchen table in his brown-striped woolen pants and webbed leather suspenders over his long-sleeved Stewart tartan flannel shirt, rolled up enough to see the red flannels underneath.

Mr. Blessing carefully followed Dalia's instructions as his finger dragged down the recipe card, like a pilot scrutinizing a preflight checklist. The special formula for holiday bread was measured, spilled, sifted, stirred, slopped, poured, and slipped into the hot oven. While the first batch was baking, they mixed the second batch. With the second batch baking and the first batch cooling, Mr. Blessing started cutting the wax paper to size while Maggie snipped the red and green ribbons to length.

There wasn't much conversation as they worked, just occasional comments by Maggie and an odd grunt by Horace Blessing. But by the time Mr. Blessing was testing the temperature of the cooling third batch, he said quite matter-of-factly, "When we get that last batch out of the oven, we can make a sandwich and eat. Then we can wrap the last batch and even deliver most of them tonight!"

"Tonight?" Maggie asked. "I can't tonight. I have a Christmas pageant rehearsal at church tonight."

"Christmas pageant. That doggone ... grddrr ... stupid ... darrnnitt ... church," he murmured. "I expected you to help me deliver them tonight!"

"I'm sorry, Mr. Blessing," she said, "I thought you knew that ..."

"Didn't know!" he spit out. "Thought you was smarter than that ..." His voice trailed off. Then with more volume he said, "Stupid ... blasted ... bothersome ... superstition ..."

"Mr. Blessing!" Maggie stomped her foot, clenched her fists at her sides, and began to turn red in the face. "How dare you—" she began but let it go. Then trying to regain her self-control, she asked, "Why don't you like church, Mr. Blessing?"

Without hesitation, as if he had memorized a part in a play, he said, "I used to go. Didn't like that preacher they got in '52. And they stopped using the real Bible—the *King James*—and they changed from those perfectly good hymnbooks and got those newfangled ones. And they wasted their money on those new upholstered seat cushions. It just wasn't the same, just wasn't good anymore ... so I quit going."

Still angry from Mr. Blessing's early comments, now Maggie was stunned by this collection of, to her, unimportant issues. Cushions? Hymnals? Really? "What about the people?" she asked.

"What do you mean?" Horace shot at little Maggie. "What about those holier-than-thou bunch of hypocrites?"

Maggie had heard enough. Though her folks had taught her to respect her elders, she now set her jaw and fired back at this crusty old grump. "Well, it's like your fruit-and-*nut* surprise loaf!"

That stopped him. His mouth froze as he seemed ready to deliver another batch of church-directed criticism and just plain meanness. Then he asked, "What do you mean 'like my surprise loaf'?"

"Do you think people like your awful loaf?"

You would have thought Mr. Blessing just heard the news that America lost World War II. His jaw went slack and color drained from his weathered face while his eyes searched Maggie for some hidden truth. Mr. Blessing seemed to shake some shock off and stated, "Of course they like my loaf!"

Maggie didn't flinch. Mr. Blessing pulled himself up to his full height, stared back for a moment, and then asked with little conviction, "Don't they?"

Maggie watched him seem to shrink and grow old in that moment. She began to regret the words that had hit him like a hard punch.

With a quiet and thin voice he said, "Someone said they didn't like the surprise loaf?"

"It's terrible!" It was out before she could think about it, and once loose it just kept running. "It doesn't taste good. What everybody likes about it is that you remember them!"

Mr. Blessing sat back and seemed to shrink on the kitchen chair.

"People like the visit you make to them before Christmas. You delivering the surprise loaf is part of Christmas here in Potowasso." Maggie leaned in for the last word. "What is important is *you*, not the stupid bread."

The kitchen was suddenly very cool to Maggie McIntry. She grabbed her coat and scarf, stepped toward the door, and turned but couldn't find any words to say. She left for the church, and Mr. Blessing only made a grunt in recognition of her leaving.

The humid kitchen was quiet—just a few ticks from the stove as it cooled and the slight squeak from the screen door being irritated by the wind. But the quiet felt less about sound and more about history.

Horace scanned the room, staring at one object and then another. He paused until the past took over the present. As he looked at the old windup timer on the linoleum counter, he could see Dalia's small hand, still dusty from the flour, pick it up and give it a couple of twists. The dirty wooden spoon was now in her hand, punctuating her sentences when she was trying to make a point. He couldn't hear her, but he knew it was a scolding. But Dalia never stayed mad long. She was already smiling as she swept the random crumbs on the oilcloth with one hand into the other one cupped at the edge of the table.

Every vision brought a moment of tenderness that gave way to an old anger. He'd lied to little Maggie, and he knew it. He was angry but not about hymnals or seat cushions. It had always been about Dalia. As he gazed at the stack of surprise loaves and the red and green ribbons and bows embracing them, he could see Dalia's delicate fingers tying the bows and then tapping the loops in a finishing gesture. Horace could almost hear his wife's whisper, "there," like a benediction.

The next day, Maggie came around to help Mr. Blessing deliver the surprise loaves. They were both pretty quiet until they were received into the homes of neighbors and old friends. Then Horace would warm up and talk freely, just like all the other years. But back outside, he kept his own counsel. They finished the deliveries, and Horace politely said his thanks to Maggie and then left her on the sidewalk as he climbed up the steps to the back porch of the old white, empty house.

The evening of the Christmas pageant, Maggie prepared to be Mary in the ancient drama. The Klonderman boy was playing Joseph again. He had black-rimmed glasses and his father's blue-checked robe tied around his tiny waist. He was a bit shorter than Maggie and had a habit of bouncing on his heels as he unsuccessfully tried to stand still.

Mrs. Glowers played on the piano "O Little Town of Bethlehem," and Mary and Joseph started up the aisle toward the stable scenery on the platform. Once on center stage, Mary knelt by the manger, looking at the baby. Joseph bounced on his heels, watched the file of visitors coming to see little Lord Jesus again this year, and pushed his glasses in place with one finger.

The two shepherds also wore robes—one plaid and the other paisley. Then three wise men—well, with Amanda Coffendaffer insisting on her right to be a visitor from the East, it was really two wise men and a wise woman—came clomping down the aisle.

The lights in the sanctuary went down as "Silent Night" began the dramatic conclusion of the nativity scene. Maggie focused on the manger and babe. She noticed a bit of green and red poking out from underneath the swaddling clothes. She adjusted her vantage point enough to recognize a fruit-and-nut surprise loaf nestled almost out of sight. Mr. Blessing must have been here, she thought. Maybe he still was. She squinted at the crowd and searched the sanctuary. There he was, the old face of Mr. Blessing illuminated near the back by a candle in the window above him. Horace Blessing had come back to church that evening.

Tears welled up in Maggie. She wanted to run offstage and give him the biggest hug he ever had, but she had to finish the pageant. The light was dim, but Maggie thought Mr. Blessing's eyes were a bit wet, like hers.

After the service, Maggie found Mr. Blessing and ran to him. She thought she had a lot of stuff to say to him—maybe an apology or a show of happiness at seeing him there—but as she gripped him in that hug, she was speechless. She looked up at him, and he looked down at her. They didn't say a word, but his soft eyes and warm smile said something was very different. Hand in hand they headed for the door. Maggie was blessed by his change of heart.

Horace never missed a service—that is, until his death a few years later. At the funeral home during visitation, an older Maggie McIntry came to pay her respects. Tears ran down her cheeks, but there was also a slight smile from such good memories. At one point she found herself alone next to the plain pine casket. She set a newly baked and wrapped fruit-and-nut surprise loaf next to the reposing Horace Blessing and, with a thin, cracking voice, said, "I'll take it from here, Mr. Blessing." And she made and delivered these treats to the people of Potowasso, who welcomed this special holiday visit. They still loved getting the attention of this little Christmas blessing.

The Christmas Program

Bobby DeGlopper had the words stacked against the entrance to his mind: "No, I won't do it this year!" Those words had to come out first. Any other words would be blocked. He just couldn't say anything else this year. Last year was stupid and embarrassing, a "little kids" thing that he was bound not to repeat this year.

"Yeah. Sure, I'll do it!"

What? Who said that? Oh no, Bobby DeGlopper thought as he heard the words tumble out in that very familiar voice: *his.*

Oh no! Tell me it ain't so. But it was. How could he say exactly what he didn't want to say? What happened to his backbone? He reached back to feel his spine and decided that the problem was that it wasn't connected to his mouth. No, his backbone was connected to an empty cavern in his head that many people used to store a brain.

Bobby continued to beat himself up, but it did not change the fact that he had once again volunteered to play Joseph this year in the Christmas pageant at First Church of Potowasso.

First Church made a long production, if not a good one, out of its annual performance. It brought in one of the largest crowds of the year, and for a Sunday night that defied the odds. But that large crowd intimidated the older kids, making them self-conscious about playacting, especially in costume and alongside little kids.

"Hey, Bobby," someone shouted.

"Yeah?" Bobby replied, turning toward the voice of his older cousin Glenn.

Standing in the hallway with a mocking smile, the tall, gangly, close-cropped blonde—a shepherd type, not a wise man—waited for Bobby to approach.

"Thought you weren't going to do the pageant this year, *Booby*."

Bobby cringed at the unwanted nickname his cousin insisted on using.

"What happened?" Glenn asked. "Mommy make you do it?" His sarcasm dripped like syrup off a hotcake. Glenn was definitely a shepherd type, not a wise man—a wise *something*, but not a wise man.

Bobby was about to defend his decision to accept the Joseph part again, but he realized that the tall shepherd type was right to ridicule him for his cowardice and lack of resolve. Bobby held his tongue, shrugged—a fool's shrug—and walked away.

Glenda Glowers had also consented to doing the Christmas pageant this year. Yet for Glenda, it wasn't a mistake but a long pattern. Who could remember when she didn't play for the program? Glenda could follow the unpredictable tempo changes and cover the children's unplanned moves; she was deft at making smooth transitions when the children would take a song in a new direction or skip whole sections of a piece.

Glenda had always planned on continuing in her role as accompanist for the Christmas pageant and would have been disappointed—not to mention shocked—if not asked. But now that practice time was here, she found herself less than excited with the task at hand.

Glenda sat at her Baldwin piano at home, looking through music and trying to concentrate on the confusing pageant script, which was covered with eraser marks, smudges, arrows, and microscopic directions squeezed into the borders. Her focus kept returning to the shock of her boyfriend of twelve years, Oren, leaving town a month ago.

She was sure they were getting serious, and she had kept expecting him to "pop the question." But instead, her Oren was pursuing a "lifelong dream" of catfish farming, which she had never heard of before. He was going into partnership with his cousin Monroe in southern Mississippi, somewhere near Biloxi. Glenda had never heard Oren speak of Monroe or catfish farming; in fact, she thought the whole business sounded *fishy*. But she was trying to believe him, as he had spoken so earnestly about the gilled pot o' gold waiting for him there. He had also earnestly maintained that his cousin Monroe needed his vast business sense that he had acquired while working at Gleeder's Market as an assistant butcher—*clean-up boy*. She wanted to believe all this, because the notion that he simply didn't want to stay with her was too terrible, even if it was so clearly true.

The last postcard she received—the one picturing the NASA Test Center outside of Picayune and postmarked Houston—had tarnished the credibility of the Biloxi catfish farming story somewhat. Whatever the case, Oren had shuffled off to greener pastures, leaving her in the snow-covered hills of Potowasso.

At first, Glenda walked around in a daze from the shock of it all. That initial trauma gave way to her own personal game show— "Wheel of Forlornment." Each day, sometimes one spin of the wheel (sometimes many) would land upon various reactions. Yesterday it landed on *guilt* and *inadequacy*, the day before it stayed pretty much on *anger*; and today was the daily double of *discouraged weariness*.

Though the pageant was a lot of work, it was familiar and time-consuming, and she needed that right now. The kids could be frustrating, and there was always more effort than was first imagined ... and it was still probably better than catfish farming.

Christmas in Potowasso, like everywhere in the United States, was a mixture of childlike excitement and adult discontent. The season was a blend of ingredients: carols and cards, tinsel and advent candles, red stockings and green wreaths, nostalgic scenes from Currier & Ives, crowded malls, TV specials and church services, candy canes and snow-covered nativity scenes, and Christmas trees with both brightly covered gifts and fallen needles underneath. It was a holiday that wove together the sacred and the secular, commercialism and the religious, into one great mosaic of delight, enchantment, fun, and hope. And even if you were cold at this time of year, the holiday offered to wrap you up in its tapestry of warmth and comfort.

Mr. LaDuke, who was an accountant at the local paper mill, left his calculator and tie at his office. At the church he was the handyman. He wore a uniform of brown matching pants and shirt. He strapped a tool belt around his waist and swaggered with a multitude of tools clicking and leather squeaking. A brown cap with a pencil stuck above his ear completed the getup. Somehow in all of this authentic handyman garb, Mr. LaDuke still looked like an accountant ... but an accountant on a mission.

He had unlocked the church shortly before the Christmas pageant rehearsal was to begin the Saturday morning prior to the Sunday evening program. He witnessed the mass arrival of children, piling out of cars and into the sanctuary with the decorum of a Wild West cattle stampede. Once corralled inside the sanctuary, the little beasts complained about the cold. The sanctuary of First Church always felt twenty degrees colder than the outside temperature in the winter, just as it seemed twenty degrees hotter in the summer. Some of the children assembled jumped from their seats, screaming about the "ice-cold" bare oak pews. Sunday-school teachers attempted crowd control, while some mothers worked as tailors and costume designers, wrestling with squirming kids to try to make last-minute adjustments.

Mr. LaDuke's attention was drawn to a group of parents working feverishly on those strange wings that had been strapped to the angels. The wires that gave shape to the wings were so heavy that they also pulled the angels' blouses so that the neck opening was tight on their throats while their stomachs were exposed. The only advantage of this was that the clothing malfunction drew attention away from the wings that bounced and flopped against the back of their legs as they attempted to walk.

Mrs. Dunnberry, who supervised the pageant and was always extremely perceptive, remarked, "Something must be done about those droopy wings!"

This received a round of giggles from the girls and a chorus of false bass voices from the boys, saying, "Duh ... really ... aren't they supposed to drag on the floor, Mrs. Dunnberry?"

In the midst of this hilarity, Pastor Quark walked in, and this quieted the giggles and sarcasm. The tall gangly parson strode up the center aisle with a wide-eyed cheerful expression, which changed quickly to astonishment when he caught sight of the bizarre angel wings that the girls dragged behind them.

Pastor Quark's simple baffled words, "Oh my!" were enough to reignite the laughter and general chaos.

After some parental shouts for "quiet" and some stern looks from Pastor Quark and Mrs. Dunnberry, a semblance of order settled over the group.

Mr. LaDuke turned his attention to his masterpiece that had been generated by a question from Mrs. Dunnberry. She had asked Mr. LaDuke the question that real handymen long for: "Do you think you could make something like I saw somewhere else?" Name it, describe it, draw it, or dream it—a real handyman can do it.

Mrs. Dunnberry described a star hanging from a wire she had seen in Amosville. It that was a star suspended from the back of the church to the front on a thin cable. The star was slowly eased down toward the manger on the platform hovering over the aisle, while in great drama, the wise men followed the star up to the nativity scene. As she explained it, Mr. LaDuke's handyman mind grabbed the concept easily.

"Yes, of course I can do that!" he had said. And today he was ready to try it out as soon as he tightened the wire that ran from the beam by the ceiling in the back of the sanctuary to the eye screw twisted into the window frame behind the choir benches. He had designed, built, and painted a beautiful five-point star. It was a heavy wooden piece with a pulley fastened to the tip of one star point. The weight, he reasoned, would help keep the star steady as it rolled down the slanting wire toward the Bethlehem scene. He would add a stop on the wire when he ascertained where the star should most properly hang.

Mr. LaDuke's plan and execution of his star apparatus were good arguments for his remaining an accountant. He was only testing the fit of the pulley roller onto the wire, when it slipped from his hands. The weighty wooden star picked up momentum as it careened down its cabled course. By the time it flew over the cradle, the star threatened to burn up like a meteorite upon entry. That probably would have been better than flying through the ancient stained glass windows now shattered and lying in pieces in the snow out back. Mr. LaDuke had done well with the star; it stood proudly without a scratch, lodged in the hood of Pastor Quark's Dodge.

With no one injured (except Mr. LaDuke's pride) by heavy wings or flying stars, the rehearsal went as it usually did, leaving those in charge with much anxiety about the program. But that was the way he always remembered Christmas pageant rehearsals—never smooth and always with the uncertainty of missed parts and missing players. The angel wings had newly designed supports, a replacement star of wonder had been cut from construction paper, Bobby's Joseph looked apathetic, and a confused and weary piano player sorted her music one more time. Practice finished, and Mr. LaDuke looked up and began to await anxiously the coming performance with everyone else.

On Sunday at 5:45 PM, Glenda watched as Mr. LaDuke arrived at First Church to turn on the furnace. After a couple of minutes of wondering where Oren was celebrating Christmas this year, she pushed away the thoughts and left the warm car for the cold church. She adjusted the piano's position and fussed with the light while Mr. LaDuke added tape to reinforce the plastic sheet covering the missing window behind the evening's stage. Glenda didn't really need to practice any of the numbers for tonight; she had come early just because she was tired of being home alone thinking about what might have been and what would be.

Mrs. Dunnberry arrived and was pacing up and down the aisle, seeming to be talking to herself. She was always nervous, but to Glenda it appeared she had an extra dose tonight as she waited for children. There were always last-minute changes and repairs to be made to costumes remembered, quick trips for some forgotten, and improvisation for the new kids who never made it to a practice at all. Glenda was always amazed at how well this nervous lady actually handled it all in surprising patience.

Glenda took a mental attendance. The one missing player, Bobby DeGlopper, finally arrived. Glenda noticed that he slumped against a wall and exhibited hound dog eyes to emphasize his poor attitude. Some grandparents were already sitting and glowing during the rehearsal of "Away in a Manger" by the second- and third-grade class that seemed to have a great reluctance to actually make a sound with their voices as they sang. Nonetheless, the old folks listening heard a chorus of angels.

It was now 7:05 and the event was about to take place. The lights in the sanctuary came down and the candles in the windows became evident. Glenda began to play "O Holy Night" as the prelude to the pageant. While she played, the words ran through her head. When she silently sang "O hear the angels' voices ..." another sound gave her goose bumps. Her eyes widened as she strained to hear what seemed like voices or maybe violins, or had the stress of losing Oren finally caught up to her and she was hearing things? Then she realized the sound was coming from the wind whining among the gaps and crevices around the broken window. A chill ran up her back when she presumed the source came from that cold air finding its way to the piano bench.

Bobby DeGlopper walked reluctantly hand-in-hand with Maggie McIntry toward the plywood manger and sparse straw that was scattered around it. Bobby rolled his eyes as he recognized his cousin Glenn, who was sitting near the front, making faces that abruptly stopped as his eyes met Glenda's. Bobby's expression and mannerisms were not lost on Glenda as she played accompaniment to "O Little Town of Bethlehem" as the congregation sang.

Why she kept watching Bobby she wasn't sure, but as she saw Bobby's resistance to his part, she had an insight into the real Joseph. Maybe Bobby was acting more like Joseph, who was not in the position he had hoped for—with a pregnant fiancée about to have a baby in a strange place. The actual Joseph must have been oozing with resistance and reluctance conquered only by a message from his God.

Glenda's attention shifted to Maggie McIntry, playing the part of Mary, who knelt at the manger owning the part of an adoring mother gazing sweetly at the Christ child, while her Joseph stood nearby, distracted with an impatient hand on his hip.

Glenda then spotted the angels beginning to make their way up the side aisles, three on each side. The wings hung awkwardly low, bouncing from side to side, hitting the wall, and then surprising an audience member. Glenda suppressed a giggle as the last garland-haloed, celestial being cleared the front pew, but she hit the back of Mrs. Dunnberry's head with a wild angel wing and a terrific *thunk*! Greatly surprised, the serious woman jumped six inches off the pew with wide eyes, and then she quickly recovered to register disgust at the clumsy angel.

Again Glenda had an inspired notion. She thought about the shepherds so long ago, who were minding their own business, not expecting the arrival of the angels and probably quite astonished to hear that a savior was being born nearby. Maybe they were a bit surprised at the disruption of their life that night and annoyed, or even disgusted, at bumping into a herald from heaven that night, making a claim on their actions that night and into the future.

Glenda made the transition from "Hark the Herald Angels Sing" to "We Three Kings," noticing the wise men poised at the back of the sanctuary awaiting the movement of the star. Finally, Mr. LaDuke must have realized the impatient boys were waiting on *his* star—well, the substitute paper star. He had rigged a fish line from the star to a pulley up front to a pulley at the rear of the church, and as he tugged on the line the star began to move with little jerks. A different junior high boy sang a verse of "We Three Kings" to Glenda's accompaniment.

Finally, the new (and less lethal) star—yellow construction paper and glued-on sparkles—hovered over the manger, the child, Mary, and Joseph. Glenda's unusually perceptive mind made another jump, wondering now how many people constructed their own stars—like she had been doing—only to see them fall, get stuck, or just plain disappear. Had she created a star and lost track of the real one that had always led her successfully and been a steady source of help?

Glenda's mental meandering ceased in time to stop playing. It was the moment that Bobby DeGlopper had his one and only line. In the quiet, all eyes became fixed on Joseph for the climactic last words of the pageant. Bobby took a step forward. He took a deep breath and delivered this line with what seemed to Glenda to contain a hint of sincerity. She guessed that even Bobby dared not speak of God's gift with indifference. He spoke loudly and clearly so all could hear: "This child is born for you!"

Bobby's voice went throughout the sanctuary, but the words caressed Glenda's soul. The Christmas pageant at First Church Potowasso was probably not much different from those across the nation, she mused—a simple, annual story of average children singing often too softly and out of tune. A cute bunch of kids—some excited, some bored, some embarrassed—presented the expected: funny costumes, wrinkled bathrobes, and silly props made by janitors, bankers, and salesmen. It was a tradition of Americana as much as Christianity, a poorly choreographed presentation with no narrative surprises. But somehow, something happened that brought an astonishing spark of reassurance to a crazy world, and a touch of hope in a discouraging time.

Glenda Glowers was strangely warmed in her spirit. Mr. LaDuke had made some poor judgments but still helped pull off the eternal story. Mrs. Dunnberry worked to make children act organized and focused. Missing that mark, she made them perfectly human. And Bobby DeGlopper, always trying to show that his involvement was senseless and childish, was the one who actually proclaimed the word from God. Things that seemed like distractions and disasters at the time became part of the revealing of a savior born in Bethlehem.

Having filed her sheet music and the terrible stage notes she had received, Glenda walked out into the vestibule and mingled. She thanked Mr. LaDuke for all his work. She squeezed Mrs. Dunnberry's arm and said, "Another wonderful pageant. I honestly don't know how you do it!" Glenda started down the front steps, nearly thrown off balance by an angel wing flying from the door, and saw Bobby waiting for his folks to finish talking with everyone on earth that night.

"Bobby," Glenda began, "you did a very nice job tonight."

Bobby looked embarrassed but was able to say, "Thanks, Miss Glowers. You played real well too." He couldn't seem to hold eye contact and seemed uncomfortable and didn't know what to do with his arms.

"You know you had the most important part in the whole thing tonight, don't you?"

Bobby now held his gaze, smiled, and said, "That little line at the end? You do more than anyone. You play stuff almost through the whole thing. That's a lot more than my small part."

"I play music, "Glenda said. "It's sacred, but it's accompaniment for everyone else. I'm glad to do it. Though to be honest, I had some misgivings now and then."

"Really?" Bobby asked. "You mean you didn't want to do it? At least, not 100 percent?"

"No. I haven't been quite with it this year. So a couple of times I wished I didn't have to do it all. But now that it's done and it did its magic on me, I'm very glad I did it. How about you?"

"I didn't really want to do it either," Bobby said.

"Really! I never would have guessed," Glenda said in mock seriousness.

"I know," Bobby said with a grin. "I act kinda screwy sometimes. But I'm getting a little old to be doing this kid's stuff. Don't you think?"

"I don't know," Glenda said.

"Well, I'll tell you one thing for sure," Bobby said with great resolve. "I'm not going to do it next year. I'm not! I mean it."

"I'm sure you do," Glenda said, nodding in agreement. "And I'm sure you said that last year too. Merry Christmas, Bobby."

"Merry Christmas, Miss Glowers."

Christmas on Sunday

Calendars are seemingly innocuous pieces of paper stapled together, used mostly to keep track of the countdown to Christmas, figured Bobby DeGlopper. He had been putting large Xs through the day squares of Gleeder's Market complimentary calendar with a glossy picture of Ken Gleeder sitting on top of the meat display cooler. It was only recently that Bobby had examined the significance of Christmas, the twenty-fifth, which was in red type—not only because it was the *big* day, but it was also one of *those* days. Christmas was falling on Sunday this year!

Today, as he crossed out December 24, Bobby came to the full realization of what the calendar was telling him: "This is your worst nightmare!" The regular schedule, the time-tested traditions, the holy and sacred ritual of Christmas morning, the unbridled, full-throttled *greed-a-thon* was going to be interrupted ... by church?

At first, Bobby reasoned that it was no big deal, just an hour, a mere hesitation in the course of time. But then he considered driving time to and from the church. Add to that his folks, who were driven by social etiquette and other foolish courtesies, feeling obliged to speak with people following the service. And then there was Dad and his compulsion once in the car. "Let's drive through town and see the decorations," he would say. Precious minutes of delay could easily swell into half an hour or so.

Then the more stark truth hit that he hadn't even considered: prep time. Not only would washing and dressing eat up the clock, it would pretty much spoil the comfort of the day. What would happen to the scampering around the tree in pj's and cramming game directions into your robe pocket?

It was turning into a nightmare. He pictured sitting rigidly in a high-back chair, with shoes, his itchy dress pants, a torturously starched stiff white shirt, and his scratchy gold-flecked bow tie rubbing his neck raw. In the vision, Bobby's mother was in a stately dress and carrying a present on a silver tray, with her stride keeping pace with the "Pomp and Circumstance March" playing slowly in the background. The sun might set before that present made its way to him.

He shook himself back to reality with a resolution: *Let's move Sunday to another day and preserve the glories of Christmas!* Bobby could now understand why so many wars that were fought had at their core religion as the instigating force.

Bobby had friends who had families with great abilities to solve this dilemma with practical countermeasures: they would open presents Christmas Eve! But the DeGlopper family was not that rational; the "Family Christmas Eve Circuit Ride Extravaganza" would not be sidestepped, even for the chaos of a Sunday Christmas. Bobby thought he was like everyone else, if they would just be honest: Christmas was for presents, not for church!

"Come on, Bobby," Evelyn DeGlopper pleaded from the kitchen. "Get ready! We are supposed to be out to Grandma and Grandpa VandeVelder's in ten minutes!"

Bobby looked at the mantle clock, which showed five thirty. He knew they were to be there at six o'clock, thirty actual minutes reduced to a ten-minute threat—the mother time-exaggeration ploy. He was annoyed, and he reluctantly turned away from the present-laden floor around the Christmas tree. Bobby found his shoes, put a quick comb through his hair, grabbed a coat, went out to the car, and waited five minutes before his mom and dad came out. Though Bobby was frustrated with the inconvenience of the calendar, he had to admit that the first stop on the Christmas Eve *tour de family* was a pretty good destination.

Gram and Gramps' farmhouse was glowing with steamy windows and colored lights galore. As he opened the back door, he was assaulted by the moist hot air of the kitchen, which was overpowered by the aroma of fresh-frying doughnuts from the deep fryer. A cheery face and demanding arms pulled him to a flour-dusted apron for his "Merry Christmas" and a great big grandma welcome hug. Then Grandpa, with his poor acting gruffness and non-menacing voice, growled, "What are you doing here? Who invited you?" Then he would lift him in a bear hug, shake him back and forth, cackle, and tell him he was just kidding (as he did every year).

Then Bobby passed the table filled with food: pigs in a blanket, ham, buns, potato chips and dip, scalloped potatoes, and that fluffy red salad with Jell-O, whipped cream, and something chunky. As he passed, he wanted to grab a sugar cookie with red and green sugar crystals on top and pick a pecan half off the coffee cake ring with white icing, where red and green candied cherries shared top billing with the nuts. And then he caught sight of Grandma's homemade fudge that screamed chocolate goodness right into your brain.

In the front room stood the tree—too big for the room but too small for the decorations that occupied every branch and covered most of the green needles. The ornaments were by and large handcrafted, but a few were store-bought and had memories attached. There were knitted mailboxes, barns, and houses. Eggs were hollowed out with tiny little dream scenes inside, with gold-and-silver and green-and-red ribbons and sparkles on the outside. Christmastime animals were made from clothespins and peanut shells. This large round fir tree was a marvelous collision of work, love, art, and memories, enough for six trees, but one missing would make it practically bare.

Bobby's cousins where checking out packages, looking name tags over, and screaming when they found their own name printed next to a candy cane or a picture or a rocking horse. This was proof of Bobby's suspicion: everybody was the same, and they were all focused on the presents.

They ate … and ate … and then ate some more. The kids waited for the last bite of the last cookie, which acted like a starting flag at the local stockcar mud track. Then they knew it was present time! With this signal, Grandpa would excuse himself for some inane reason and go into the bathroom, where his Santa outfit would be waiting.

But this particular year something bizarre happened: the old familiar suit either wore out or was lost. Yet this did not prohibit Bobby's ever-resourceful granddad from making the magical transformation into Santa Claus. There was bewilderment and wonder on the faces of the kids, and everyone was pretty sure Grandpa hadn't looked in the mirror before coming out of his bedroom. But, after a moment, the shock passed, the enchantment took over, and Santa started to appear from this fashion stew that the old man had cooked up at the last moment. He wore black rubber zip-up boots, red quilted, insulated leggings and vest, and a white-and-blue terrycloth dish towel stuffed under his black Russian-looking fur cap, towel hanging down kind of covering his chin. "Oh! It's his beard!" Grandma shouted as her imagination caught up with Grandpa's ingenuity.

"Ho, ho, ho, merry Christmas." Grandpa VandeVelder reached for a bass voice. "Oh, we have some children who have been good boys and girls this year." To Bobby, this accomplishment seemed to exhaust old Santa, and as if in confirmation, Gramps declared, "Someone else is going to have to pass out the presents. Whew! I'm getting too old for this."

Another piece of evidence. Even Santa knew it was about the presents. Even he could be replaced, but the presents had to get delivered.

Suddenly the magic of Santa's appearance flirted with the admission that Santa was only Grandpa disguised. Bobby and his cousins froze, staring at this old man in a really bad costume. It was like reality and imagination were fighting for domination. But no one—neither child nor adult—wanted the enchanted ruse to end.

Like a good elf, Grandma VandeVelder stepped into the moment and said, "Santa needs to rest in Grandpa's chair before he resumes his busy schedule to other good girls' and boys' homes."

Santa said, restoring the myth, "Yes, that's right. Santa's never too old. Santa just needs a little breather and off I'll go to finish my rounds!"

With the tradition saved, Bobby, his cousins, and all the adults got to the important thing—opening their presents. They screamed, laughed, giggled, and made other sounds and gestures as another gift was unwrapped. Everyone, young and old, said thank you. And all the kids were ready to move on, but Bobby was annoyed as his folks then began grown-up talk, that boring talk that seemed to go on and on. Bobby started watching the clock. Bobby was willing his folks to grab a last hug and get going. Finally, with Bobby nearly going crazy, ready for the next stop and the next present, they left for their next stop—Aunt Corrine and Uncle Jacob's house.

They pulled into the cement driveway, scraped clean of snow with the precision of laser surgery. The house was sided in gray asphalt shingles and had white trim. It was very neat even though very old. There was an old yellowing plastic snowman in the front window, and on the porch Uncle Jacob had wrapped lights around the porch swing. Bobby had heard his father say more than once that Uncle Jacob didn't really know what to accent in his holiday decorating attempts.

Bobby and his folks walked in the back door and noticed that it was a little cooler inside than out—Corrine and Jacob were frugal. Bobby reluctantly relinquished his coat. "Furnace go out?" Bobby asked as he rubbed his arms. His father answered his question with a stern look, shot like a bear cuffing a wayward cub.

The kitchen was nicely decorated with a Christmas dish towel hung on the oven door handle and a holly candle ring encircling a stubby mint-green candle. Bobby remembered this candle from the spring deco candle ring, the summery daisy candle ring, and the earth-toned fall candle ring. Mint green was kind of a multiseasonal all-purpose color for Aunt Corrine. (More likely it was a cost-saving matter.)

Bobby examined the kitchen table and the depressing and sparse holiday fare: a lopsided cake, a bowl of chips (no dip), and a punch bowl filled with a new tasty treat. Bobby listened to Aunt Corrine tell his mother how she had found this new recipe for holiday punch in a magazine she scanned while in the checkout lane at Gleeder's Market. She revealed her justified resistance to spending $1.75 for a magazine, and she had a darn good memory and could certainly remember this simple recipe. As Bobby took a gulp, his taste buds or his mind or both were confused. He'd stop concentrating on the conversation, but it seemed to him Aunt Corrine had mentioned orange juice, Lipton tea, and V8 juice, spiced with nutmeg. His aunt's mental copy machine must have inadvertently scanned a portion from an adjacent recipe in *Good Housekeeping* or something.

Bobby and his folks moved through the kitchen and entered the next room in this holiday house of horrors—the living room. Aunt Trina, his mother's sister, was rolling her eyes and giving her sister knowing looks. Her reaction might have been because of the Christmas tree squatting in the far corner. It was fat and short, not really coming to a point, looking more like a Christmas bush. Though fat, it was anything but full—just a few boughs stuck out here and there like they couldn't escape with the rest of the frightened branches. Bobby counted fourteen very large and old bulbs, which weighted down the branches. They looked to Bobby like fishing poles that had caught a whopper that was diving for the bottom. He noticed eight large and sad ornaments trying their best to cover the open spaces. They failed. On what was apparently the top of the tree was an angel on which one wing was taped. Four presents were accurately set around the foot of the tree. There were four presents, one for each kid. The adults had lost the will for presents here, and Bobby couldn't figure out what they did for Christmas without gifts.

The living room was clean and neat, not cluttered with a lot of Christmas things. A few cards sat on the coffee table, some faded plastic poinsettias were stuck in with the living growth of a planter, and a set of blue and green ceramic letters spelled "N-O-E-L" (well, they did before Bobby rearranged the letters to spell "L-E-O-N"). The problem, Bobby thought, with this Spartan approach to decorating was that it left almost no place to hide the gross punch you had tasted and now carried around seeking some cloaking device.

Uncle Jacob was big on background music. They listened to Boots Randolph and Patsy Cline over and over. Bobby heard a few comments and little jokes about the country twang, but Aunt

Trina really objected, or maybe it was the whole atmosphere of this particular family visit. Whatever it was, Aunt Trina snapped. She went so crazy that she did what the whole DeGlopper family tried to always avoid—she told the truth.

"Corrine," Aunt Trina began, "this punch is dreadful. You must have made a mistake with it!"

The place went silent. Aunt Corrine whirled and stared at Trina and then turned on the whole family gathered. "Is that what you all think?" she asked with disbelief.

Everyone was stunned, probably by a combination of truth and audacity. The silence was answer enough. Bobby just hoped it wouldn't delay the present exchange.

"Well, no one has to come here if they don't appreciate my attempts to make things special!"

"Boy, I'd hate to taste the stuff that isn't special!" Bobby said quietly to his cousin Leonard, Aunt Trina's oldest. He tried to hold back a laugh. He got a bit of control and then looked at the cup of punch in his hand and lost it. Leonard was trying to drink the "special" punch, and now it was exiting him in *special* places.

"Nice nose fountain, Lenny!" Bobby chuckled.

"Oh no, not on the carpeting!" Uncle Jacob shouted.

"Lucky you weren't out on the porch swing," Trina's husband, Uncle Butch, said. "You could have been electrocuted!"

Laughter was spilling out from all sectors now, and it wasn't really the medicine that was going to calm Aunt Corrine down. She walked into the adjoining bedroom and slammed the door so hard that her favorite picture of her beloved deceased miniature schnauzer named Scooter fell over and took with it Bobby's dad's cup of punch he had stashed behind it.

In trying to catch the falling picture of Scooter, Uncle Jacob was able to actually deflect it right into the Christmas tree, taking out two irreplaceable ornaments and one very large green lightbulb. With this portion of the family Christmas pretty much destroyed, the DeGloppers found it an excellent time to move on. They said some hasty good-byes and left some mad relatives and a heightened fear of new recipes, but Bobby was still hungry for the next present.

During the short ride, heading for what Bobby believed to be the final stop on the Christmas Eve circuit, he thought about how awful it would be to spend his whole Christmas at Aunt Corrine and Uncle Jacob's place. They always had bad food, almost no decorations, and a meager amount of presents. And on top of all that, they weren't really any fun, unless you like very slow car crashes.

Bobby so wished the night would end so he could wake up and go downstairs in his own house with all the packages and ... *oh. I forgot*, he said to himself as he remembered, *tomorrow is Sunday.* Then out loud he said, "Do we have to go to church tomorrow?"

Without hesitation, Bobby's dad replied, "Yes, tomorrow *and* tonight!"

"Tonight! You mean we're doing church tonight and tomorrow morning?"

"That's right. No discussion."

Mr. DeGlopper was still struggling with the strain of the last visit as he pulled into Velma Starkweather's driveway. Velma was someone they called "aunt" but really was a cousin or great-cousin or something on Evelyn DeGlopper's side. She was old but very modern: modern appliances, late-model Cadillac, trendy clothes, and artwork that must have been expensive (because it seemed meaningless and ugly to Bobby's eyes).

Velma had no traditions, as far as anyone knew, and that was part of the fun of visiting on Christmas Eve for Bobby. She did not decorate the same way any year. Whatever she thought was in vogue was what she seemed to use. This year it was simply silver.

There were white appliances in Velma's white kitchen, and everything else was chrome or stainless steel. Some silver garland was hung around the windows, and a silver wreath was on the back door.

In her front room was a new artificial tree. Yes, silver. Shiny silver boughs held strings of clear miniature bulbs. Crystal ornaments finished that colorless monument. A lovely silver nativity set was sitting on the white Steinway piano, reflected from the set of mirrors over the couch. Chrome and white leather chairs were placed on the white plush carpeting that looked as if Bobby and his family were the first to ever set foot on it. On the clear glass and chrome coffee table was a silver platter with little cookies, and they took your breath away—cookies dusted with white powdered sugar and bright-red candied cherries in the middle. The red of the cherries drew your attention. It was like Dorothy's first glimpse of color when she left Kansas and landed in Oz.

It wasn't long in this stark decor of Aunt Velma's before Bobby was actually craving color. Even Aunt Corrine's mint-green candle would have been a spicy addition in this color-drained world.

"Boy, Aunt Velma," Bobby freely offered, "this is *really* different."

"It's simply elegant," Mrs. DeGlopper said.

"Makes you feel like you're living in a dream!" Mr. DeGlopper added with what Bobby thought was a certain smugness for coming up with that little phrase.

Bobby could see that everyone had learned their lesson for the night: no more truth—give compliments. Bobby saw the present under the tree; it was the only one, and he knew from years past it was for them.

"Would you like to open your present now, Bobby?"

"Sure, Aunt Velma. Is that it under the tree?" Bobby asked, knowing it was a stupid question, as it was the only package there. This was as close to not getting a present while literally being named on the tag. Only one gift for the whole family. What gift could excite parents and kids? None.

"Yes. Why, let me get it for you," Aunt Velma offered in her formal way of speaking and then with matching formal movements. Bobby marveled at how she could move and even bend down to pick up something while her back always stayed straight and her chin was held high.

But what was most puzzling to Bobby was that he could never tell if Aunt Velma was angry about doing stuff for you or happy about it. Apparently, it was not fashionable to show any feelings at all. It dawned on Bobby that there was a sterile kind of personality in Velma that was reflected in this year's decorative style. What Bobby wouldn't give to be opening up one of his gifts in his own house, with all its color. Even its messiness on Christmas mornings seemed like heaven.

The gift Velma handed him looked like it had been wrapped in tinfoil, and it had a white bow. Inside was a box of candy. *Whoopee.* Bobby couldn't read the label, because it was some foreign junk that was expensive, rare, and probably yucky.

"Thanks, Aunt Velma," Bobby said, wondering what to do with it.

He was rescued as his father added, "Let's save it for tomorrow, Bobby. That will make it even more special. Thanks, Velma."

Thankfully, this gift letdown was done, and it was time to go. The roller-coaster ride of this night's visits was just about done. Bobby rode in silence in the backseat of the car. As they passed houses with lit windows and cars parked on the street, he speculated about the chances of everyone's relatives being equally as weird as his. *Couldn't be.*

The DeGlopper family walked into the eleven o'clock Christmas Eve service and found seats halfway up. Bobby turned around and scanned the room, looking at each person and wondering if he could tell by appearance which ones had already opened their gifts. Probably the happiest ones, he guessed.

As people walked down the aisle to find an open pew, Bobby thought how different all these people were. Rich, poor, funny, dull, enthusiastic, and very weary. Some of the kids he looked forward to seeing, and some, like Eddie Crawford, were real nerds. There was Bobby's Sunday school teacher, Mrs. Kroos, who knew everything in the Bible and some more stuff that should be. There was Mr. Traverson, who taught the high school class and spoke a lot, but even the kids knew didn't know squat. Pastor Quark was up at the lectern, making sure everything was in order as he fussed with quick, nervous little motions. He kept pushing his glasses up on the bridge of his nose and adjusting his tie.

First Church of Potowasso was a collection of odds and ends to Bobby. It was odd that they were all so odd. Could it be that some of the people he thought peculiar were the ones others thought were normal? Then it struck Bobby as a possibility that, to some of those odd people, maybe *he* was odd.

Right then Aunt Corrine and Uncle Jacob stepped through the doorway, followed closely by Aunt Velma wearing a fancy silver fox coat.

"Wow!" someone said as she strolled by.

"Get a load of that! Must have cost a pretty penny!" someone closer to Bobby said.

Pastor Quark cleared his throat, and yet it still cracked as he began. "Welcome to First Church" was all he got out, seeming to lose his train of thought as Grandma and Grandpa VandeVelder walked in none-too-quietly.

Bobby tried to catch the eyes of everyone he had visited that night and gave them a smile when he did. They smiled back, except for Aunt Velma, who nodded stately. Little scenes went through his mind for each person he looked at. They were a funny bunch of folks. Funny, but they all gave gifts, some better than others for sure, but gifts nonetheless.

Then as he was scanning the sanctuary, he noticed Jimmy Fisset from his class, who seemed to be doing much the same as Bobby. He looked around, held his gaze a moment on his aunts, his uncles, and his grandfather Fisset, and with each person Jimmy shook his head as if almost in disbelief. Maybe everyone was a little strange, especially if you knew them well enough, Bobby reasoned. It seemed Jimmy was as fascinated by his own family members as Bobby was.

Yes, my family is different, but not too different! My family's not extra strange or odd. Maybe none of the many people here tonight were weird, just unique. These people had a variety of traditions, styles, ways of speaking, and personalities. They certainly had different backgrounds, tastes, and experiences. They were here at First Potowasso, not because they were alike, but in spite of their differences. This young philosopher, Bobby, was getting tangled in heavy thinking—so heavy that forgot to be anxious for the service to end and Christmas present time to be here.

Bobby's contemplation ended as his attention was drawn to Pastor Quark, who began paging through the hymnal he held as he addressed the congregation.

"I am glad you all received the summons by God to be here tonight. We are called to gaze at the Divine One this evening, who comes to us as a baby—"

And give us a reason to have presents, Bobby thought to himself.

Bobby listened as he looked around and thought about how different they all were. They probably held little in common other than the town of Potowasso and the love of presents.

Pastor Quark continued, "We have been called together to praise a God who would unite us in one heart."

Again Bobby's thoughts about the gifts were interrupted by more deep thinking. They didn't hold so much in common but were *held* in common by a God who came as the most different of all, a God who was also this child, Jesus—a Lord who does not count himself better but lays it all down for weird people. He seemed to accept eccentric people, whether cheap or generous. He accepted those who overthought and who imagined conspiracies—as he had. Bobby even figured Jesus loved those guilty of focusing too much on presents and lost track of the real gift of Advent, as he had. No matter how different each one was, no matter how they got along, no matter how far from perfect they were, not one of them could match the uniqueness of God, who became a person. Bobby decided it was a perplexing world in which he lived. He was just really glad that God was in charge of making things, not Aunt Corrine.

Pastor Quark said, "Let's all stand and sing number 171 in the brown hymnals, 'Joy to the World.'" Bobby stood with all the other people of First Potowasso, and he began to realize the joy of being a part of his family and his church of simple, unique, weird, and lovable people who with him called Potowasso home. He grudgingly admitted to himself that presents weren't the only thing people thought about, and nor were they the only thing he should think about.

When Bobby hit the hay that night, he got to thinking about tomorrow being Christmas and Sunday. It didn't happen very often, and maybe it was one of those lessons his mother and father spoke about, which life could be full of. He really loved all those people, even more than the gifts. Yet Christmas was extra fun, even when it got messed up with Sunday.

Christmas Blackout

Pastor Quark was told that this was one of the coldest Decembers in Potowasso history. On December 14, it hit zero degrees Fahrenheit. And, as it was said commonly in these parts, "Then it started getting cold."

As if reading his thoughts, his wife, Mary, asked, "How cold is it supposed to get, honey?"

He was squinting at the thermometer outside the window when he said in his terrible impression of Johnny Carson, "How cold did it get?" Then in answer to his own question, he said, "It got so cold that Mr. Laraby, the lawyer, had his hands in his *own* pockets!"

Mary laughed.

"It got so cold that hitchhikers through Potowasso were holding up *pictures* of their thumbs!"

Now she groaned.

"It got so cold that even *property taxes* froze!"

Mary said in her terrible Ed McMahon impression, "That's cold!"

The thermometer read eight below, and the windchill made it feel like twenty-five below. Potowasso had already received fourteen inches of new snow since midnight, and the wind kept stirring it up. As he turned away from the window, Pastor Quark wondered how it was affecting others in his parish. Later Pastor Quark would find the answer to his musing.

Lude Swattleberg had a dairy farm outside of town, and the harsh weather didn't change the fact that his herd needed to be milked. He walked into the frigid barn and found the herd huddled at the far end of the shelter. Even with extended utters, the cows seemed reluctant to move toward the milking stations. Bessy, the old matron of the herd, finally gave way to Lude's prompting, which was essential if he was to gather the rest of the herd. But just as Bessy stuck her head through the stanchion, the lights flickered and then went out. The power had failed.

Lude went to his small supply house and brought his power generator to life. He switched on the circuits to his barn and house. He had enough power to run his milker pumps and his lights so he could see what he wanted to see.

At the same time, at Gleeder's Market, the lights went out and a number of last-minute shoppers were marooned in the back aisles, frozen in the sudden darkness. Mrs. VanderHoff tried to keep going, only to run into the pickle section of the glass aisle—the smell of gherkins and dill nearly overwhelmed her. Blanch Pickford was reaching for a tomato at that moment and put her thumb right through a beefsteak shipped in from Southern California. Owen Bell, ironically, was shopping for lightbulbs at the time.

Manager and owner Mr. Gleeder, like a civil defense volunteer, quickly turned on a flashlight to guide his way to the office closet that contained an old crank-operated cash register. "Neither rain nor sleet nor gloom of night will keep me from my appointed profits." It was an old Gleeder motto.

While the power failure hit the Swattleburg farm and Gleeder's Market, the power failed at First Church too. Miss Glenda Glowers, the pianist, was practicing her music for the night's service. She had it all memorized and was proud to think that tonight there would be no sheet music on her piano. Suddenly in darkness, Glenda continued playing but slowed a bit. She knew the music and knew the keyboard and could persevere in the dark fairly well. Finishing the chorus of "Hark the Herald Angels Sing," she stood in the pitch black. She reached for the first pew to find her bearings in order to find her way to the office wing, where the secretary or the pastor must be working.

Mrs. Pike, the church secretary, was just about to run the evening service bulletins when the power went out. Pastor Quark heard her say a naughty word, followed by "Oh, not now!" He knew just what she was thinking, that the bulletin should have been ready to run yesterday but that he hadn't picked his sermon title yet. She probably thought he was a thoughtless laggard who was putting her in a bind. And he knew she would remind him at the first possible opportunity that though he was the holdup, she would be blamed. He could hear her predictable dictum: *But who am I to complain? I'm only the secretary.*

While Mrs. Pike was sputtering out in the outer office, Pastor Quark was having his own dilemma. He had decided, after much consternation, to do a first-person sermon. He had never done one before, but he thought he and his congregation had become a bit predictable and dull. They had been using the same format for every Sunday service forever, it seemed, and the Christmas Eve service was no different. Usually his secretary could simply reproduce the previous year's bulletin, only needing to change the date at the top, but this year he decided to be different. *That's where change gets you*, he thought.

In a move Quark thought would be quite startling, he replaced the opening carol, "O Come, All Ye Faithful," with "O Come, O Come, Emmanuel." Then in further wild abandon, he decided to put the choir number *after* the Words of Assurance and *before* the reading of the Law. (The choir had always followed the Law. This change almost felt like the breaking of a religious code!) But then he made this most outrageous decision, to do a first-person sermon.

He chose to be a shepherd and tell the nativity story through the eyes of this rusticated herdsman. Not only would he speak from this rusticated viewpoint, but Quark had asked his wife to produce an authentic costume from which to portray his pastoral character. The big problem had been deciding if he should wear his glasses. It was not at all authentic, but of course being blind as a bat wasn't going to help a preacher who had never preached extemporaneously. Also, he had not memorized a sermon even once.

He was attempting to fold his shepherd's head mantle to cover the frames of his glasses. In the midst of a crucial fold, the lights went out. Pastor Quark dropped his glasses and then kneeled down to retrieve them, only to crush them with his right knee. Mrs. Pike must have heard his even-naughtier word he howled in exasperation. She had never heard that kind of language from him before, and hopefully she would not believe he could have said *that* word.

After several tries with tape, Pastor Quark decided that he could not make his glasses hang together aligned enough so he could see, and the tape would really look silly with his costume. But what would he do to see his masterpiece of a sermon? The lights just had to come back on by service time! He could accept no other possibility.

Mr. LaDuke—banker by day and super-church custodian by night and weekend—was in the basement hauling out the last prop for the Christmas scene on the church stage. It was the beautiful star that he had made a few years ago that had traveled along a wire from the back of the sanctuary to the front, as the wise men would follow it. The first time out it tragically got loose and sped down the wire so fast that it didn't stop over the stable but kept going past the holy family, beyond the back altar, and through the ancient (irreplaceable) stained glass windows, and flew until it impaled itself in the hood of Pastor Quark's car. The star was now stationary and hung from a single wire above the creche. The drama of the moving star was replaced by the visual enhancements—some glitter and little lightbulbs on each arm of the star run by battery.

Enough about the past. This year Mr. LaDuke was most proud of the new animals he had cut out of plywood and painted in painstaking realism. He was most proud of his enormous one-humped dromedaries. The elegant golden halters and the big brown eyes nearly brought the Asian beasts to life. To Mr. LaDuke, the scenery was his greatest achievement and (though he didn't need any praise) it was what got him the most acclaim from his fellow members of the congregation.

First Potowasso held an eleven o'clock service every Christmas Eve. As Elder Welker always liked to say, "We've done a Christmas Eve service every year since we began doing them! Maybe even longer." Mr. Welker drank a little at the holidays.

Even though the leaders gathered at Elder Bruggink's home for an emergency meeting, the thought of canceling the service because of the power outage was not seriously considered by anyone but Pastor Quark. And predictably, Elder Welker argued, "We've done Christmas Eve services before we had electricity, so why not have one after we have electricity?"

Pastor Quark looked at Elder Welker and was sure the man had been drinking and therefore wasn't making any sense. Or maybe if Quark had a little nip he might just be able to understand his elder. The thought vanished as the power came back on at about ten o'clock.

After a few minutes of light and the sound of the furnace kicking on, they voiced assurances that the power was on to stay and the service could go on as planned. And so they dispersed with a great feeling of providence and good fortune. Things were coming back to normal around town. The group left the house to life as usual, and preparations for the Christmas Eve service were back on track. But Pastor Quark was sure that the events surrounding this year's service would become legend. *The Christmas Eve service that got saved by God's special interest in them. The miracle of the timely healing of the power grid.* Or something like that.

Lude Swattleberg finished his chores, cleaned up, and got a fresh pair of dungarees for the night out. Mr. Gleeder finished his counting with the aid of his electric adding machine, with great relief. Not to mention he was a bit giddy about the big number on his "total" column. Glenda Glowers was relieved to be playing her part tonight with noticeably *no sheet music* needed, even with *all* the numbers she had to play. Mrs. Pike could run her bulletins and, because of her programs, Christianity would survive.

Pastor Quark paced nervously and checked his watch so often that his wrist was beginning to hurt. Nerves were normal for any service, but this was the big night and he was especially anxious about his first-person sermon. The lights comforted him, knowing that he didn't have to deliver his sermon by memory. And he was very thankful that the impressive costume would be a glorious sight for all to see.

Quark peeked out from the altar door to see that Mr. LaDuke was making a last-minute adjustment to his nativity scene for the most advantageous effect. He then walked backward out of the sanctuary, fairly enamored with his visual masterpiece and ready for the unveiling tonight. He could see that the church was mostly full. The parents of the kids were early to drop off their little actors and actresses, singers, and exceptional memorizers of biblical passages. The grandparents had filtered in, and those persistent latecomers were a little bit less late on such a special night.

Quark went back to his study for the customary elder prayers before the service. Mr. Gleeder and Mr. Swattleberg left the study first to ready the collection plates. Mrs. Pike was running off some last-minute extra copies of the bulletin and rushed them to the narthex. Things were set, and people were in their places. Elder Bruggink ascended to the lectern to welcome the folks, make a few announcements, and give a few nods of appreciation to the many who helped make this special service possible.

Elder Bruggink grabbed the lectern with both hands, looked out on the jam-packed sanctuary, opened his mouth, and ... the lights went out.

"Not now," Pastor Quark heard Mr. LaDuke exclaim.

Mrs. Pike said, "Oh, my!"

And all heard Elder Bruggink shout, "Doggone it!"

A little whimper of despair came from Glenda at the piano.

"Holy mackerel" was heard from Mr. Gleeder.

"Holy *something else*" came from farmer Swattleberg.

And Quark heard an enormous scream of pain come from his own lips as he missed a step coming up the back way to the platform and cracked his shin on a stair tread made of a very sound piece of oak.

There were a few gasps from the audience and some giggles from the kids all lined up at the back, ready to make their entrance as the Christmas program unfolded. The parents and grandparents were sighing at the thought of missing the chance to see and take pictures of the kids, as they would prove to be so cute, smart, gifted, and just generally exceptional.

There clearly was a collective sentiment of anguish as the lights remained dark. Pastor Quark was disappointed that his costume would go unnoticed. The deacons worried about the evening's collection getting reduced by loss of guilt, as no one would see them skimp. Mr. LaDuke feared the loss of visibility for his props. Glenda's pride of memorization was threatened. Parents and grandparents were deflated by the letdown of no spotlight on their kids and grandkids. The majority were certainly thinking about the power outage and wondering, *Why now?*

The flickering candles in the widows didn't make much of a difference on the black hollows of the Potowasso church. Certain despair had settled on the folks attending that night. So much for all their work and all their talent; so much for the effort of dedication and the pain of commitment, not to mention the earlier impression about the intervening providence of God. Quark wondered what the Lord had against the poor saints at First Potowasso but quickly pushed this possible blasphemy away. He recovered with a more controlled reasoning that there were just times things inexplicably don't go your way, and this was plainly one of those times.

As the darkness continued, prolonged past any notion of a short-term outage, one thing stood out—Mr. LaDuke's battery-operated star. As the handyman was later fond of saying with a chuckle, "It was the one *bright spot* in the program." But at the time, a more profound comment came from little Tommy Klonderman. As Pastor Quark listened to the various comments of disappointment and wrestled with his own feelings of regret, the high-pitched voice of little Tommy cut through all the discouragement with these words: "Well, at least the Jesus star is shining!"

"That's certainly true," Pastor Quark said to nobody in particular. He gazed at the Jesus star shining and the manger below lit up by it. Somehow, in the cosmic moment, in that otherwise gloom of a building without power, a message was being sent to him and his flock, a regular bunch of folks. Whether they consciously understood it or not, there was a message of humility and of common sense being proclaimed. *Everything else,* Quark thought, *everyone else must be in the shadows while the star of Bethlehem shines in the night.*

Pastor Quark's eyes were becoming accustomed to the dim light of the candles, and he could begin to recognize the various people in the sanctuary who had worked so hard for this night. All had different expectations from what they were now experiencing. As he quit thinking about what he was disappointed about, he imagined what the others were thinking. All were probably caught up in their own hopes, expectations, and this one event with that simple phrase from little Tommy conveying a different message to so many people in so many ways.

Pastor Quark opened the back door all the way and stepped onto the stage area. He quickly realized that everyone's focus was on that star with those accompanying words: "Well, at least the Jesus star is shining!"

He pulled his attention from the star long enough to look at Glenda Glowers regaining her poise and beginning to play—by memory and without sight—"O Holy Night." It began quietly and with little missed notes, but Pastor Quark was warmed as she gained confidence and the music picked up volume and tempo as wrong notes decreased. The music swelled, and the old carol came alive in the glow of that lone shining star. The congregation began to sing in the dim sanctuary while they watched that star.

O holy night! The stars are brightly shining,
                                           a few began to sing along …
It is the night of our dear Savior's birth.
                                           some more folks joined in …

Long lay the world in sin and error pining,
'Til He appear'd and the soul felt its worth.
>   most everyone sang out ...

A thrill of hope the weary world rejoices,
For yonder breaks a new and glorious morn.
Fall on your knees! O, hear the angels' voices!
>   now they boomed full blast ...

O night divine, O night when Christ was born;
O night divine, O night, O night Divine.

Pastor Quark was very thankful that light was still shining and never more sweetly than that night of the Christmas Eve blackout in Potowasso.

A New Year's Resolution

Many people make resolutions at the New Year. *Resolution* is just a secular term for the church's word *repentance,* you know. You don't hear about repentance so much anymore. The older folks make fewer resolutions as time goes on. They know few really make the changes they wish they could. So instead of making resolutions, lots of folks go directly to guilt and shame, avoiding the brief exertion of discipline. But in Potowasso, the young and the old make resolutions. It has been that way for as long as people can remember. This is a story of one of those years.

Most New Year's Eve parties that take place in Potowasso are dedicated to announcing people's resolutions. Determination is the climax of New Year's Eve parties in Potowasso, well ahead of romantic gestures at the stroke of midnight. It is much more likely that people will "cross their hearts, hope to die, poke a needle in their eye" at the initial moment of a New Year than kiss anyone.

In fact, it is more than a custom in Potowasso. Making a resolution for the New Year borders on the obsessive. Many a Christmas joy has been ruined by the anxiety of the impending New Year for those who have yet to come up with a viable resolution. It's nothing you want to wait on. You should start thinking about it right after Labor Day, and hopefully by Thanksgiving you will have come up with a bad habit to break or a good habit to begin.

Now some avoid the annual problem by sticking with the same old resolution year after year (which seems to reward failure somehow). Others feel the need for a different one every year, whether or not they are able to keep it. This compulsion to formulate a new resolution year after year gains in difficulty as the years roll by. For example....

Bastian Yonkman had successfully come up with thirty-seven resolutions, which was coincidentally the number of years he had been within the contract of marriage to Jacoby. (As an interesting side note, though it is neither spoken nor a formal rule, more of the married seem to have this need for resolution. Old Duffy Welscott, for example, had never been married and never seemed resolved to change anything in his life. Now if that is proof that only married folks follow this tradition, or if it is perhaps just indicative of why Duffy had never been married, it was not clear. Nevertheless, Bastian Yonkman had successfully navigated thirty-seven anniversaries and contrived thirty-seven original resolutions. But the well had run dry.

Bastian was smart and disciplined. Early in each year, he began thinking of the next resolution and was pretty well set by summer. The last few years it had taken much more time to arrive at the decision. Last year it was Halloween before he settled on his resolution—which, by the way, was to shine his three pair of good shoes weekly.

This was the secret of Bastian's success in thinking up resolutions. He would examine his life and find something not regulated and regulate it. Waiting for the new year to begin, his resolution had always been tougher for Bastian than actually coming up with the resolution.

But this year it was different. It was the day before New Year's Eve and he had not yet come up with the resolution that would propel him into the new year. Not that he couldn't come up with one, but he had trouble coming up with a resolution that he was satisfied with. Lesser men might accept any old resolution, but not Bastian Yonkman—he had pride. And, as is often yoked to pride, he had a problem. And his problem was growing as the days passed, moving ever closer to the new year without a respectable resolution. That's what he was burdened with as he stepped out into the garage.

Stories from Potowasso

Now, Duffy Welscott, the old bachelor, lived next door to Bastian and Jacoby Yonkman on Wilmont Street. Oh what contrast between Yonkman and Welscott—polarity at its utmost. When Bastian thought about his neighbor, he vacillated between pity and disgust. He wasn't sure whether to feel sorry for Duffy or be shocked most of the time. To Bastian, Duffy was the epitome of the undisciplined and disorderly.

The Yonkman house was a large two-story home built when it was fashionable and affordable to have gingerbread around the eaves and elaborate spindles marking peaks and corners. All this extra garnishment was painted a rich chocolate brown, while the window and door trim was a lighter but a complementary tan. The clapboards of the house were white, a bright and flawless white. The shrubs lining the driveway and under the front window were mounded with snow, but the uniformity of their shape was not hidden. The driveway itself was bare concrete, as was the front sidewalk, the cement walkway to the front door, and the steps and porch. Yonkman had shoveled, salted, swept, and perhaps used a surveyor's scope to position the sharp edge where snowy yard met dry concrete with obsessive precision.

Duffy Welscott lived in a much more recent dwelling but seemed much worse for wear. It was brick, where the brick was not missing, which was on both sides of the garage door, about bumper height. And that may have explained Duffy's inability to close the garage door, though the stuff that was crowding the doorway, like a volcano about to erupt, wasn't much help. The white trim around the single-level house was screaming for attention, and one gutter was bent at a ninety-degree angle due to a load of ice it could no longer support. The end of the driveway had been shoveled, probably to remove the accumulation left from the snowplow. But the rest of the drive was a series of ruts and chunks of dirty ice that had fallen from the wheel wells of his old International truck.

It was garbage pickup day and the reason Bastian had stepped out into the garage. He wheeled his brown garbage can down the driveway, leaving it precisely at the road's edge and off his driveway, on the little patch of shoveled space he had tidily reserved for his garbage can as it waited to be emptied. And within ten minutes of the pickup, Bastian would have it back in the garage on that piece of cardboard near the back door.

Bastian noticed that his neighbor, Duffy, had forgotten it was garbage day again. Duffy was under the hood of his truck when he must have heard the whisper of Bastian's garbage can wheels rolling down the immaculate drive. He was engrossed in looking for something, perhaps the oil cap. At the sound of Bastian hauling the garbage out, he jerked suddenly, cracking his head on the raised hood of his old Dodge half-ton.

"Ouch!" Duffy said, rubbing the back of his head. He disappeared for a moment into the morass of his garage and then reappeared dragging his brimming, dirty, and squeaky garbage can through the pits and over the outcroppings of ice and snow along his driveway terrain.

Bastian eyed his neighbor and asked, "Did you hurt yourself, Mr. Welscott?"

Duffy chuckled. "Just banged my head on that darn truck, Yonk."

Bastian hated that little nickname his neighbor used for him.

"Thanks for reminding me to bring the garbage out."

Bastian nodded but did not speak. He was busy examining his neighbor: disheveled, in need of a haircut, and needing new glasses, or at least new frames so they wouldn't require the white tape to hold one bow on. Bastian noticed one of Duffy's black rubber boots was buckled up, and the other was tied together with twine. This was not a sign of poverty, for he knew Duffy worked at the paper mill as a foreman. And without a family to support and the inheritance of his house from his parents, he must be comfortable. No, Bastian knew that the old boots just represented an unfathomable disregard for order and a certain standard of comportment.

Duffy took a bad step and fell backward into the snow, while his garbage can fell over with the lid opening and the remains of a week's worth of pizza boxes, fried chicken tubs, and wadded Burger

King wrappers spilled out. "Ouch!" he said for the second time that morning.

Stepping carefully toward his fallen neighbor, Bastian asked, "You all right, Mr. Welscott?" Then he tried to help the man up. The dilemma was attempting to help without touching him. Duffy struggled like an upside-down turtle—a two-hundred-pound disheveled turtle—in the deep depression he had made on impact.

With Bastian's help, Duffy finally was able to get to his feet, only to immediately fall again as he fumbled to grab his fallen garbage can. Bastian wasn't sure how to help Duffy, seeing that he had now lost a boot that remained in the snow, with his shoe still inside and his sock flapping in the wind, snagged off by a broken buckle.

"Shoot," Duffy chortled, "I oughta make a resolution to get a new pair of boots!"

Bastian wanted to ask if he really thought the solitary cause of the problem here was footwear, but he resisted in an attempt to retain his neighbor's tenuous dignity.

Duffy struggled into his sock, shoe, and boot, while he used Bastian's shoulder for balance. "Remember when the garbage man used to actually walk up and get your can, dump it, and bring it back?" He exhaled with almost a whistle. "Boy, those were the days! Didn't know how good we had it."

As Bastian watched Duffy grapple with his old boot, he couldn't help but think of how many things his neighbor could use for resolutions. Bastian could not count the possibilities contained in this unruly life. He could begin with some resolutions about personal hygiene, apparel, outside maintenance, organizational procedures, and, though he had never been in his neighbor's house, Bastian was fairly certain the inside habits were no less in need of some modifications. Duffy Welscott was a mountain of disorder deposits not yet mined, a virgin forest of chaos, a garden teeming with the undisciplined weeds of the unplanned.

Bastian watched Welscott wince in pain as he attempted to put weight on his freshly shoed foot. And he watched his neighbor fall again into the snow.

"Uh-oh," Duffy said, "I did somethin' to my ankle here."

Bastian got behind his rumpled neighbor, grabbed him under the arms, held his breath so as not to inhale odors or germs, and helped him to his feet. "Did you sprain your ankle, Mr. Welscott?"

Gradually putting some weight on the ankle, he said, "I think I might have, Yonk."

Just what he didn't need, Bastian thought, being in this situation of obligation, when he had so many details in his own life to take care of. Reluctantly, Bastian heard himself say, "I'd better take you to the doctor." He knew it was the right thing, but he wished he could avoid it or at least wait for the garbage truck to come so he could put his garbage can back where it belonged.

"Maybe I should," Duffy said. "You sure you wouldn't mind?"

Bastian attempted to smile in reassurance and said, "I would not mind. In fact, I insist."

Bastian pulled his spotless, gold Crown Victoria out of the garage, parked at the end of Duffy's drive, and helped the big man into the front seat.

"Nice ride, Yonk. This is like new, but what is it? A '94?"

"A 1993," Bastian corrected.

"How fast will it go?"

"I don't know," Bastian said.

"You don't know?" Duffy asked incredulously. "You mean to tell me you never opened this thing all the way up?"

"No," Bastian answered a bit defensively. "It's not good for the engine, I'm sure. And I have no place in which it would be legal to drive above seventy."

"Wow," Duffy coughed. "You're ... a very careful person, aren't you, Yonkman?" It didn't sound like a compliment to Bastian.

"I am mindful of the law and careful with my car and other possessions." Bastian knew he was moving past defensive and heading toward anger. "I was raised to take care of my things."

He signaled, made a slow right-hand turn onto Franklin Street, and continued, "Such as my driveway, which saves me from accidents, such as yours." Bastian knew that he had made a score but felt immediately guilty for it and said, "I'm sorry, Mr. Welscott. That was uncalled for."

"No it wasn't, Yonk!" Duffy said excitedly. "That's what I mean. You feel somethin', you gotta just say it. You gotta, right?"

"I have no right to be disrespectful," Bastian said.

"Ya weren't disrespectful. Ya just had a burr on your saddle that you had to get." They were passing Klingman's Bakery and Duffy quickly changed subjects. "Hey! How 'bout some doughnuts?"

"Doughnuts?" Bastian asked, incredulous. "I thought you wanted to get to Dr. Brown's."

"I do, but it can wait. I'm hungry, and I could say hi to Marge at the counter. You pull in and I'll spring for 'em," Duffy said, licking his lips.

"But where would we eat them?" Bastian asked.

"In the car," Duffy said matter-of-factly.

Bastian stared in disbelief at his rider and then scanned his car's spotless interior.

"Oh, I see. You don't eat in the car, do ya, Yonk?"

"I've found no reason to."

"Shoot!" Duffy said. "My car looks like a landfill, with all the wrappers and stuff. I bet I eat in my car more than in the house." And Duffy laughed.

Bastian was speechless at this thought. Not only did this Neanderthal eat in his car, he made a mess of it and laughed about it.

Bastian drove past the bakery.

Duffy's head swiveled as he followed the bakery that went by. "Maybe on the way back?"

Bastian pulled into the parking lot, which served Dr. Brown's office, the dentist's office, and Heidi's Flower Box. "I'll go in and get a wheelchair for you."

"Hey, that's nice of ya, Yonk. You been awful thoughtful."

Bastian returned with the wheelchair, only to find Duffy using cars for support as he worked his way toward the flower shop. "Where are you going?" Bastian asked, easing the wheelchair behind Duffy.

"Just dawned on me that it was my sister's birthday yesterday. Thought I'd wire a bouquet or somethin'."

Bastian sighed with frustration.

Duffy hunched his shoulders. "You wanna do that after the doctor's too?"

"*Yesss*," Bastian pronounced it with precise exaggeration. "If we do these other errands, let's do them after we take care of the primary reason for our excursion—your ankle."

"I get a real kick outta how you talk, Yonk. You never get out of control. You're always ... I don't know ... careful—no, censored. Like the preacher or your mother was always watching you. That or the missus is using a might too much starch in your shorts. Is that it, Yonk?" Duffy laughed shamelessly at his own joke.

Bastian cringed at the slang and the critique by *him* of all people. But he said nothing. He just counted to ten silently and pushed his neighbor through the doorway of Dr. Brown's.

While they waited for the doctor, Bastian attempted to take advantage of his time by deliberating on his resolution decision. His brow was pinched in thought, and his jaw was tight as he clenched his teeth in desperation. What on earth could he change for the better? What would this year's resolution be? He was getting a headache, and he could feel his neck muscles setting up like drying plaster of paris.

Bastian was beginning to hyperventilate, as he worried not only about the resolution but about other tribulations: his empty garbage can setting out by the road, the salt on his car from the ride here, crumbs that would get on his upholstery if he allowed his neighbor to eat a doughnut in the car, and the time he would be forfeiting if he had to wait for Duffy to choose and order some flowers for his sister. And what would be the next distraction? Duffy Welscott drove him crazy.

"Somethin' wrong, Yonk?" Duffy asked.

"No. Well, yes. I have not come up with a resolution yet. And I need one by tomorrow." Why was he telling Duffy Welscott his business?

"Maybe I can help," Duffy said.

"I don't really think so, Mr. Welscott. But thank you for your interest."

"Yeah, sure. Anytime, Yonk," Duffy said.

"Mr. Welscott?" the nurse called and then held the door open as Duffy rolled himself through the doorway. "Lookin' good today, Lois," he said to the matronly looking nurse and winked.

As the clock continued to be consumed by this unscheduled activity, Bastian watched Mitch Hagerstone walk in. He checked in at the counter with Lois and then came over and sat next to Bastian.

"What are you here for, Bastian?" he asked.

"I'm just here with Duffy Welscott." Bastian rubbed his temples. "He had an accident this morning."

"Duffy hurt?" Mitch asked. Then, with a fondness that Bastian thought was usually reserved for close family, he declared, "He is such a great guy. Always has time for you. You're lucky to live next door. My car got stuck a couple of weeks ago and good ole Duffy stopped and helped, even though he was already late for work. What a guy."

"Yes. What a guy," Bastian said dryly.

"You don't look so good," Mitch said. "Maybe you should see the doctor."

"I'm fine," Bastian said, forcing a smile. Then to change the subject to what he knew anyone and everyone would have on their minds, he asked the very married Mitch, "By the way, have you decided upon your resolution this year?"

"Yeah," the older man said as he examined the magazines on the table. "I guess I'll resolve to get a little more exercise this coming year. How 'bout you?"

"Don't know yet," Bastian said, shaking his head slightly. "I've pretty well organized most things. I'm not really sure what I have yet to correct or repair."

Just then, Duffy burst out of Dr. Brown's office, along with a bellow of laughter from Dr. Brown. The doctor slapped him on the back and promised to talk with Duffy soon. Duffy made some inaudible comment to Lois, the nurse, who cackled and wiped her eyes.

Mitch stood, extended a hand to Duffy, and said, "What on earth are you doing here? You crazy varmint!"

"Doc Brown needed a new set of tires, so I came to donate to the cause."

Bastian watched Mitch fall apart with laughter, and the nurse squealed with delight as Dr. Brown pushed his door open again, smiled broadly, and exclaimed, "You old goat, quit tattling on me!"

"Sorry," Duffy said. "What were you doing, holding your stethoscope up to the door?" There was more laughter, some tears of joy, and more smiles than Bastian thought were necessary. He sat with his back straight, hands folded in his lap, and dignity in every square inch of his body, a man saturated with resolve and discipline and looking for even more as he remembered his lack of a resolution.

"Hello, Bastian," Dr. Brown said.

At the utterance of his name, Bastian felt every smile fade, every laugh hush, and every eye dry. Bastian searched the room, not moving his head to draw attention to his awareness of the uncomfortable change.

"Mr. Hagerstone," Dr. Brown said soberly, "I believe you are next."

"Nice to see you, Bastian," Mitch said and then followed the doctor.

Nurse Lois sat with a stoic expression. "Say hello to Jacoby for me, Mr. Yonkman."

"I will," Bastian replied and held the door open for Duffy and the crutches he had acquired.

On the way home, after stopping at the flower shop and the bakery, Bastian and Duffy approached a party store with the sign "Third Base—Last Stop Before Home."

"Hey," Duffy said, "let's stop and get some pickled bologna and hear Lester's latest story. You know he always has a good story."

"Mr. Welscott," Bastian began, tight as a high E-string, "I have really wasted enough time. I have many things to do and some decisions to make."

Duffy said, "Oh, sure. I'm sorry, Bastian."

He couldn't remember Duffy ever calling him by his given name before and wondered what it meant. They drove silently the rest of the way home.

Bastian pulled into Duffy's driveway as far as he could.

"Wanna come in a minute, Yonk?" Duffy asked.

Using the nickname he had always disliked somehow relieved him and relaxed some tension that he hadn't realized had built in the silence.

"You could see the bird feeder I'm puttin' together for Mrs. Vanderbeek across the street."

"You may not have any plans today," Bastian said, "but I have a long list of tasks to complete and responsibilities to fulfill." And then with a reluctant civility he added, "I hope your ankle heals quickly."

"And happy New Year to you, Yonk!" Duffy offered.

"Hmmm" was all Bastian could get out.

About to slam the door shut, Duffy leaned in and said genuinely, "Thanks for your help, Yonk. And if you're still looking for a resolution, you might think about cutting yourself some slack, quit a few of the 'things,' and add more *people*. Just a thought. You can really—"

Bastian cut him off. "Thanks for your input, Mr. Welscott." And with that he was backing out of the drive.

Bastian tossed and turned all night, troubled by the impending New Year and his lack of resolution.

Bastian and Jacoby went to Ike and Irene Coffendafer's, as usual, played canasta, and drank fruit punch with rainbow sherbet thrown in as the clock moved toward full attention.

"Heard you took Duffy to the doctor yesterday," Ike said over a fistful of cards.

"How'd you know that?" Bastian asked.

"Duffy told us this morning."

"Where did you see him?"

"Oh, he saw our kitchen light on as he was headed to Mrs. Vanderbeek's with a bird feeder."

"He's on crutches, for Pete's sake," Bastian said. "He walked through the snow on his crutches? Why on Earth would he do that?" Bastian shook his head.

"He wanted to know if we could use some salt for the sidewalks. He knows we always have company on New Year's Eve. Duffy's always stopping by. If not here, someplace. Like he doesn't have a care in the world ... except everyone around him."

At nearly midnight, people started divulging their New Year's resolutions. Bastian passed his turn. He was distracted. Finally, everyone else having disclosed their resolutions, all eyes fell back on Bastian, who was having trouble concentrating on what the others were saying.

"Well, come on, Bastian. Out with it. What's your resolution?"

Bastian looked at them but was reliving the day's adventure with Duffy Waldorf: the good-natured clumsiness, the spontaneous change of focus, the way he talked to everyone, and how everyone seemed happier after he arrived. He could see people's faces light up when they heard or saw Duffy. He couldn't help but grasp his neighbor's relentless alertness to any possible needs or likings of everyone else he encountered. And this last act of fighting his way through the snow on crutches to see if the Coffendafers needed some salt on their driveway? Bizarre. Neighborly.

Then, as if he had awakened from a wonderful dream and was almost surprised that they were there, Bastian said, "Okay." He squinted as he mulled over his decision, and then gathered himself, relaxed in a way he never knew he could, and said with contented resolve, "My resolution is ..."

He paused while everyone waited, watching him intently as that inside grin he was feeling seeped outside.

"My resolution is to break the speed limit while I eat doughnuts in my car!"

He watched as they all looked at each other, quite puzzled, and then back at him. But he realized with some surprise that he didn't care if they understood, and he didn't care if he really understood. He just liked the feeling and began to chuckle to himself.

"And maybe purchase some pickled bologna."

Irish Green

Potowasso is a small town in the Midwest, with an Indian name but mostly Dutch descendants and a smattering of poor Englishmen. And the only group of residents who were more suspect than the English were the Irish.

Saint Patrick's Day creates minimal excitement in a little community, like Potowasso. Only one of the five bars sells green beer, and the Windmill Flower Shop shifts its window display from a Valentine's Day theme to Easter and spring, as if the month of March is a mistake not to be bothered with. In fact, the four corners of Potowasso's main business district is noticeably barren of any of the Irish regalia found in so many other places in the middle of March.

Pastor Quark was making these judgments as he walked from his church study to the market for some skim milk. He laughed to himself as he thought about how the bulk of residents here wouldn't recognize a symbol of Saint Patrick's Day if it slithered out from under a rock as a flute was being played. To the folk here, clovers were part of the problem for lawn care fanatics (of which there were more than a few). A rather harsh critique crossed his mind: you would think that you were saved by faith *and* a manicured lawn. Theology mixed with horticulture—an odd thought even for Pastor Quark.

He knew other tokens of the Irish holiday went equally unrecognized. He'd heard Grace VanderBeek ask Mr. Nederhood at the drugstore why he had those "funny little dwarf-pilgrims in green hats on the candy display so long after Thanksgiving." He told her he wasn't sure and they just came in a candy company promotional kit with that "kettle of corn chowder attached to a rainbow."

Saint Patrick's Day normally slid by unnoticed by most of Potowasso's citizens. But if a person left town by the old River Road to the north, one couldn't help but pass O'Mally's. Shawn O'Mally was a third-generation transplant from the town of Kilkenny in the county of the same name. O'Mally was not only proud of his heritage—which completely baffled most—but he flew a Notre Dame flag, which appeared, to most of his Go-Blue!-U-of-M–worshipping neighbors as equivalent to a golden calf.

Most in town were nervous about being seen entering this establishment, because he sold a modest amount of beer, ale, wine, and liquor. No one asked for a bag when they bought the odd loaf of bread or bottle of ketchup; they preferred those watching to know exactly what they had purchased. Carrying a brown paper bag from O'Mally's was paramount to an admission of "that devil alcohol" consumption. In Potowasso proper, that could nearly send you to the dunking stool in the center of town.

O'Mally admitted that his adult beverage sales were the difference between making a living and not. But most of his liquor customers came from Milo, a small town four miles to the east, which oddly enough had a party store where most of their customers come to from Potowasso. Alcohol sales were the commodity, which encouraged the most cultural exchange between the two villages.

O'Mally was an outcast, not only because he sold booze, but because his tonsils were no stranger to its soothing consumption. He had a small butcher shop at the rear of the store, where O'Mally spent most of his days, while his wife, Caoimhe (pronounced *kee-vah*), stocked shelves and ran the register. It was rumored that by three o'clock in the afternoon on the average day, it was not safe to buy meat, because O'Mally often leaned on the scale simply to keep his balance, and the unsuspecting customer often paid a couple of dollars more per pound just for O'Mally's equilibrium.

Maggie McIntry, half Irish and half Dutch, was sent by her mother down to O'Mally's for two pounds of ground beef and a loaf of Butternut Sandwich bread. The old brass cowbell clanked as

Maggie pushed through the door. Caoimhe greeted the youngster while she continued to stock the candy rack.

"Good day to ya, young Maggie!" Caoimhe said. "What can we help ya with today?"

Maggie pulled out a small piece of white paper and read it out load. "Two pounds of ground beef, low on fat and light of the butcher's hand, if you please."

Caoimhe O'Mally nodded without any annoyance.

"And Mom wants some bread," Maggie said, stuffing the little note back in her pocket.

O'Mally started scooping meat from the tray in the case while Caoimhe checked date tabs on the bread, giving Maggie the most recent. These were good people who wanted to serve the town and make a modest living. If it weren't for a strange prejudice, it would have had a better record and a bit more profit from the start. But an odd event would soon knit these Irish upstarts and the established Dutch into partners.

Old lady Simpson had died a few years back. Her husband had been the owner and operator of the large paper mill across the river. Simpson Corrugated was the largest employer in the community since 1931. High school kids got summer jobs cleaning the pits under the steamrollers, and adults worked with the beaters, drove jitneys, and shoveled pulp.

The Simpsons were rich, not only in Potowasso estimates, but anywhere. They had a huge wooded lot just west of the business district, on the south banks of the Katamacasi River. On that huge parcel sat an honest-to-goodness mansion—an imposing two-story Elizabethan structure with corner towers, balconies, and a pavilion-roofed carport. But Mrs. Simpson had outlived her husband by thirty years, and the mansion had outlived any caretaking for about the same length of time. The paint had peeled, boards warped, shingles deteriorated, and foundation stones shifted. The place had gone to seed—crumbling, fading, and cracking. But when the residents of Potowasso looked at this overgrown eyesore, they still saw reflections of greater and grander days. There was pride that, at one time, one of their own had made it, succeeded in a world that usually sidestepped small towns and rural people. The Simpson mansion was the local seal of approval—an endorsement of Potowasso as a legitimate player in the world of accomplishment. And that was why its future demise cut to the heart of a simple people and bridged the gap between the Irish and the Dutch.

Judge Cynthia Costass of the appellate court had the county's present version of wealth and power. She had bought the Simpson place at a tax auction and held it for a couple of years. Now word was that she proposed to tear the manor down and replace it, no less, with a Laundromat and parking lot. The rumors of leveling the mansion circulated and created murmurs from Potowasso, which duplicated hysteria in most places. The judge was "a crazy, old, greedy hag, who ought to be run out of town on a rail"—if they still had one. How low could avarice take someone? Was she serious? Raze the Simpson mansion and replace it with some coin-operated Kelvinators? Unbelievable!

At a town meeting, set to discuss and clarify the issue, the town council assembly room was packed with residents—angry and curious alike.

Judge Costass presented her case without much emotion. She almost seemed bored with the facts: she owned the property legally, the real estate was comprised of commercially zoned land, and all local ordinances had been obeyed to the letter.

In contrast, an angry, red-faced Mr. Gleeder, the grocer, voiced what appeared to be the majority view: "We don't care what some legal mumbo jumbo says. We know what's right. And this ain't it!"

A wave of agreement rolled across the jam-packed room, holding tight to the hope that popular opinion could overturn what statutory regulations could not.

There is something about a common enemy, which unites the staunchest of adversaries. The council chambers were full of Dutchmen, a sprinkling of English, and the two Irish families who lived within the city limits of Potowasso.

Bastian Yonkman spoke about the "commercialization of America," while his bride of thirty years, Jacoby, looked on with great admiration. Duffy Welscott didn't think TV commercials had much to do with tearing down old buildings but said if it was helpful, he would be willing to pay closer attention. Clarence VanHuizen warned the citizenry of air pollution and traffic jams resulting from all the people west of town who would be attempting left turns on West Allegan Street. King Dixon said that his hardware store might lose clothesline business, while Abe DeKam feared the ruination of washer and dryer sales from his appliance store.

The debate went on among those present—mostly money or attractiveness being the foundation of the defense. And some, like Claudette Klonderman, believed it just didn't "seem right," which must have sounded like a better argument in her head than when it was verbalized. Judge Costass appeared to be pretty much unaffected by all the verbiage bouncing around the chambers that evening. Then Shawn O'Mally spoke up.

It was no secret to those who witnessed his words, and his less-than-steady bearing, that O'Mally had been the best customer of the day for Seagram's amber nectar. He steadied himself with one hand on the folding chair in front of him and one on his wife's shoulder, swaying like a hula dancer on Maui. He gathered his thoughts as best he could while under the influence of alien persuasion. He slurred an obscure opening remark: "It's all about your shoes, Judge. All to save your precious, shiny shoes ..."

A few snickers, many bewildered looks, and a couple of rolling eyes met Shawn O'Mally's as he continued to speak. "This reminds meeee ... of somethin' my graaaaandfaaather told me about," O'Mally stammered. But once he got into the flow, his lingual control sharpened. "Once the largest and most important and historic monasteries in Ireland, St. Mary's Abbey, founded originally for the Benedictine order of Savoy in 1139." With a dramatic sweep of his arm, which almost took him to the mat, O'Mally continued. "It became Cistercian eight years later and remained such *until* it was dissolved by Henry VIII in 1539, in his greedy little rush to get his hands on monastic lands and treasures."

"Get to the point, for goodness sake," roared the impatient Mayor VanHuizen.

"Here's the point ... Your Excellency." O'Mally bowed facetiously while giggles and snickers washed over the hall. "In 1676, the sanctuary, the main part of this big, old, beautiful—did I mention it was big? Anyway, this grand structure ... a piece of art—sacred art, I would add—provided nothing more than a quarry for stone used in the construction of Henry's precious Essex Bridge. And not only that, but all that remains of the cloister itself—you know, the monk house, which was a magnificent edifice in its own right—the only evidence that it stood in Essex ... is that they have unearthed old Cook Street on the farside of Liffey ... and that's it. For the king's shoes, the stones that once formed the quarters for those who gave their lives to the church ... are nothing but a cobble street ... a buried street no longer used."

O'Mally seemed to run out of fuel, slumped a moment, looked around, and appeared puzzled as to his location. Then with a lurch he stood straighter, starched with determination.

"All I know is that once you knock history down ... you begin to walk on it. You forget about what it was and what it meant. You have to, or you could not stand to step on it to stay out of the mud. That's what you are doing, Judge. You're going to bury history so you don't get your shoes muddy."

Then after a pause in the quiet of the room, O'Mally finished. "Well ... I suggest you stop worrying about the tops of your shoes ... and think a moment about the soles ... or soul—S-O-U-L, if you like!" With another elaborate wave of his hand, O'Mally's wife led him out of the crowded town hall.

There are probably few things that truly bother us, as when things we don't like are all jumbled up with what we do like. And nothing creates more emotional conflict than within our religious conscience. The good citizens of Potowasso did not care for O'Mally's public inebriation, and for that they wanted to reject his words. But there was the conflict—his *words* eloquently conveyed what they could only think, while his condition conveyed what they rejected ... or at least tried to hide.

Pastor Quark, who had remained quite invisible up to this point, stood awkwardly and offered some words of spiritual wisdom via an illustration. "To me it's like Black Forest cake—I love cherries, and I love chocolate cake, but I am not so wild about putting them together."

That sparked a mumbled debate in the back of the room about the merits of this culinary combination.

Pastor Quark was able to ignore the minor disruption and continued now with his ace-in-the-hole Bible talk. "It was this same type of conflict that turned Pharisees into speechless fools. When Jesus told the Good Samaritan story about compassion and rescue, he let the hero be a despised Samaritan, while the righteous priests were the apathetic, self-protecting weasels."

That last turn of phrase felt a bit like cursing, and the good pastor was a trifle uncomfortable with it. And then a more distressing notion hit him: he was, in fact, siding with O'Mally and in some strange way supporting the sale of liquor. He saw the townspeople who did not attend his church nod in agreement with his comments, but the folks from First Potowasso seemed conflicted. A deacon in the crowd was wincing, and a longtime member and chair of the Women's Guild was definitely scowling. Though strong drink was not a specific taboo to the denomination, there was a strong reluctance to endorse its consumption.

Pastor Quark sat down and realized that something had changed. In that simple act of supporting O'Mally, a new precedent was threatening. Long-established social tradition—categorizing people by the wisdom of prejudgment—was being reversed. The Irish were prone to excessive drink, as lawyers and judges were apt to be cruel and unfeeling. Quark wondered where it would end if a person couldn't make lightning-quick conclusions about any situation by simply cataloging the participants. And yet he had just stood with an Irishman—and not just any Irishman, a drinking, bar-owning Irishman. What next? Be friendly with Episcopalians?

Quark sat motionless while his eyes searched the room for an answer to this dilemma. In his visual quest, he spied Spinster Walters, an ancient one from his own flock, sitting directly in front of him. She was smiling and nodding at him. It was encouraging.

He would have thought she would feel obligated to chastise his unseemly Irish alignment.

Then Spinster Walters whispered conspiratorially, "It's all right to act upon the issues now and again. Mr. O'Mally will be Irish tomorrow, and you can be against them all day." She beamed with knowing tolerance and said sweetly, "Tonight it's okay to save the old mansion even if it means standing with that drunken bum from Kilkenny."

Quark almost got whiplash as he did a double take to make sure those words came from Spinster Walters. They did.

Pastor Quark recalled a story he was told by an elder since deceased. It was about a fellow telling the elder that he didn't want to join First Church because there were so many hypocrites going there. The old saint had replied, "Well, you go find a church without hypocrites and join it! Then they'll have one."

Pastor Quark became aware of the meeting room again and the ongoing cacophony of few opinions and many heckles: Dutchmen agreeing with Irishmen, sweet old ladies voicing wisdom and then talking trash, and a judge being judged by a cantankerous jury of nonpeers.

In the end, Judge Cynthia Costass did not build the Laundromat, and the reason was probably the mixture of a well-lubricated speech by Shawn O'Mally and the biblical reflections of a confused minister. A couple of things changed after this town assembly. More people were seen frequenting O'Mally's—not necessarily for the booze (the booze they still bought over in Milo), but bread and milk sales went up and they knew enough to continue to buy their meat early in the day. The other change was that people never tracked mud into the house or walked over a simple bridge without recalling that special meeting around Saint Patrick's Day.

Pastor Quark had a new appreciation for the complexities of human nature, the lessons that could be learned from the strangest people, and a personal awareness of those with the best of intentions acting with shades of hypocrisy. But he still bought his beer in Milo.

Spring Break

Spring is such a hopeful time. The whole world seems bursting with promise.

Some of that feeling is the natural response of overcoming the challenges of winter, the relief of leaving those extra snow- and cold-related chores behind. Daring to put the snow shovel back in the toolshed, wearing regular shoes to the car instead of galoshes, and listening to the news on the car radio while the engine warms up, and not standing in the cold, scraping ice off the windshield.

The optimism of spring may also be traced to God's symphony of creation—as if every living creature and every botanical organism is on the verge of multiplying. Creation takes center stage; beginnings are brightly colored buds on trees, and large-eyed, clumsy calves and colts investigating a new world alongside their mothers. Brown fields turn green, and gray skies are transformed to blue. Days lengthen and the night recedes. How could we help but be hopeful and just a little giddy, when life is begun or renewed right before our senses? Spring is an annual genesis being written by God, a promise proclaimed by all living things.

That was the mind-set of Claudette Klonderman, the forty-four-year-old art teacher, as she walked to the Potowasso Public Library on Mill Street. It was as if she had been given new glasses, which magnified every bud, sprout, and bloom, while the colors of this fresh world intensified to a surreal splendor. Claudette heard the birds chirping and peeping and all those other encouraging sounds they manufacture. The air she inhaled carried a blend of the most diverse aromas that she could imagine—familiar and yet new at the same time. What a glorious day to be alive!

She hesitated at the door of the library, unwilling to leave the burgeoning world for the artificial lights, the musty tomes, and the relative silence of the aisles and stacks inside. One last deep inhale and then she pulled open the door and stepped in.

Leaving the light-hearted Claudette with the dim linoleum, Mill Street continued and became, at the city limits, Mill Road, a paved road without gutters. That, in turn, became a dirt lane. Over a small hill and through a cool shady hollow, one could turn down a long two-track driveway that ended at the back porch of Edgar Eagan. Only three miles from the library, you would have thought you'd traveled to another country … even a different season.

Edgar, wearing his bibs and flannel shirt, pushed open the screen door. Instead of swinging, the door fell to one side, only attached by the bottom hinge, which twisted and threatened to give way itself. "Riber-rotin," he muttered, an untranslatable curse to regular folks, but it seemed to mean something to Edgar, because he had been using that same jargon most of his fifty years. He kicked at the base of the flimsy door, only to find the corner with his shin. Another "riber-rotin" and the rather large man stepped onto the last wooden step off his back porch, which seemed to disintegrate under his rubber boots. Edgar fell forward, catching himself with a big, bare hand in a small mud puddle. He hated spring.

The thaw made a quagmire out of the driveway and barnyard. Everywhere he looked, there was a chore to be done, something to be repaired, or a mess to clean up. This stupid screen door was just another entry on the long list of tasks, which seemed to literally grow with each step he took.

Edgar removed the old pipe that leaned against the barn door, minimizing the gap in the doorway. He slid the door along and off the track, for the stop had stopped stopping. "Riber-rotin!" he bellowed, scaring the barn cat, Patches, off his bed on a straw bail.

Giving in to the malicious design of fate, he mumbled, "What else?" only to be promptly answered by the telephone ringing back at the house. He ran for it, leaping over the broken steps of the porch, grabbing the doorknob of the back door, but not quite turning the doorknob far enough around, before his shoulder, carried by his momentum, broke through the door's windowpane. "Double riber-rotin!" He snagged the receiver. "Hello." The dial tone was the only answer.

He hated spring.

Claudette found a beautiful new book of American poetry. She sat on the bench just outside the library and browsed though the book. She came upon one of her all-time favorites—"Trees" by Joyce Kilmer.

> I think that I shall never see
> A poem lovely as a tree.
>
> A tree whose hungry mouth is prest
> Against the earth's sweet flowing breast;
>
> A tree that looks at God all day,
> And lifts her leafy arms to pray;
>
> A tree that may in Summer wear
> A nest of robins in her hair;
>
> Upon whose bosom snow has lain;
> Who intimately lives with rain.
>
> Poems are made by fools like me,
> But only God can make a tree.

Claudette closed the book, hugged it close, and gazed at the maple trees along the street, promising to burst with leaves soon, and maybe they would lift their leafy arms and begin to pray.

Edgar tacked the heavy plastic sheet over the back door, threw the hammer to the side, and heard the dogs' water dish shatter. "Riber-rotin!"

He walked to his old Ford half-ton pickup, opened the driver's door carefully, slid in, and turned the key in the ignition. To his surprise, it started on the first crank. He gingerly put the truck in reverse, cautiously backed up, cranked the wheel, shifted into first, and pulled out onto the dirt lane.

A couple of minutes later, Edgar found a parking space in front of King Dixon's hardware store. Luck was finally with him, he thought. And then quickly he cringed, worried that any positive notion was just asking for a new disaster. He strolled gingerly into the hardware store and pulled a list he had prepared from his pocket.

Claudette was about to head for home when she remembered she needed to pick up a new clothesline, post, and hook while she was downtown. King Dixon's Hardware was just around the corner.

Mr. Dixon was cutting a replacement window while Edgar Eagan checked the prices of putty. He tipped his hat as Claudette Klonderman walked into the store.

"Good morning, Mr. Eagan," she said with such joy.

"Yeah, whatever," Edgar grunted back.

Claudette was nothing if not quick-witted. "What can possibly be wrong on a perfect day like this?" she asked, now seeing the muddy sleeve of his worn flannel shirt.

"Oh yeah," Edgar said. "This is a real winner of a day!"

Just then, King Dixon emerged from the back room with the pain of glass wrapped in brown paper. "What else can I do you for, Edgar?"

Mr. Eagan replied, "Need some of this putty, couple of hinges for a screen door, a few half-inch nuts and bolts, and a short piece of angle iron."

King Dixon's wife, Florence, stepped out of the one-step raised office that overlooked the store and smiled at Claudette. "What can I help you with, Claudette?" she asked.

"I need forty-two feet of clothesline," she said. "And a hook to fasten it to, and a post ... one of those special green ones," she said. And in saying it, she watched Mr. Eagan seem to wince.

"You probably mean a pressure-treated post," King offered.

"Whatever," Claudette replied.

"We don't carry lumber, Claudette," Florence said. "You'll have to get that at the lumberyard."

"Oh my," Claudette said. "That's a long way to walk."

As Edgar listened, for some dark reason, he was delighted by Claudette's frustration. It was a tiny cosmic acknowledgment that the universe wasn't against only him. Even this silly woman with her cheerful attitude and idiotic smile sometimes met with an inconvenience.

"You got your truck, Edgar?" King Dixon asked.

"Of course," he responded, before he understood the connection.

"You got time to take Miss Klonderman here to the lumberyard?"

"Riber-rotin," Edgar said under his breath. "I suppose so," he said out loud.

"No," Claudette said, "you don't need to go to any bother for little ole me."

"It's no bother," Edgar said with the enthusiasm of a limp noodle. "I'm parked right out front. I'll be glad to take you, Miss Klonderman."

"Oh, call me Claudette. Please."

Wally's Lumberyard was just across the river, north of the Potowasso business district. Edgar slid the four-by-four into the back, climbed back in behind the wheel, and waited for Claudette to return from paying Wally. In his impatience, he fiddled with his radio, trying to find some station that wasn't playing a dumb rock-and-roll song or that boring longhair music. He found some guy whining about a lost love, a missed train, and a broken guitar. *Now that's music.* He listen, waited, checked his rearview mirror, thought it needed some adjusting, and promptly broke it right off the bracket. "Riber-rotin!"

Claudette climbed into his pickup, holding a yellow receipt and carrying a syrupy grin. "You're so kind, Mr. Eagan. How will I ever repay you?"

"Know how to fix a mirror?" he asked, tossing the detached part back into the bed of the pickup. He held a finger up, waited, heard the clatter of broken glass, and said, "Well, my day is complete!"

"Pardon me?" Claudette asked.

"Aw, nothing. Just not a real good day," Edgar confessed to himself as much as to his passenger.

Edgar pulled into Claudette's driveway and pulled the post out of the back of the truck. "Where you want it?"

"It goes where that broken one was," she said, pointing to a ragged stump behind the house. "Could you stick it into the ground while you're here, Mr. Eagan?"

"*Stick* it into the ground?" he asked. "You don't just stick these ... oh, never mind."

Edgar dug out the old post remains, replaced it with the new one, and tamped the ground around it to hold it fast.

"There," he said as he checked his watch to see how much of this rotten day had slipped away—a good hour, for sure. "That should do it," Edgar said, wiping his hands on his dungarees and turning around, only to see Claudette holding the new hook toward him with the innocence of a small child.

Edgar exhaled through pursed lips, giving in to the folly of any sense of control he'd salvaged up to this point in his day. "Why don't I just put that in for you too," he said, taking it from her hand.

After a brief search in the garage and finding a spike and hammer, he returned to the post, made the pilot hole with the nail, and began twisting the hook into place with a pair of rusty pliers he found in Claudette's garage.

"You're so kind, Mr. Eagan," she said.

"Call me Edgar," he replied.

Claudette blushed. The color of her cheeks seemed to signal a long unused emotion in Edgar. *What was that strange feeling?* he asked himself. *Attraction?*

How could this wallflower, Claudette—who made Popeye's Olive Oyl look voluptuous—suddenly look attractive, even kind of pretty? A few decades as a bachelor did alter one's perception, he supposed.

"Edgar," she said shyly, "would you like to stay for lunch?"

Now, it was Edgar's time to turn red. "Shucks," he said with a shrug, "I'd love to have lunch with you, Miss Claudette." He smiled for the first time in about fifteen years. He felt like a schoolboy again.

Absentmindedly he twisted the hook into the new post. Even as the clothesline hook broke off in his hand, the hardwood resisting too much for the cheap hook, he did a strange thing: he laughed.

Claudette, watching him, looked crestfallen at the mishap, and she said quite delicately, "Riber-rotin!"

Gourmet Hash

Pastor Quark was working on a sermon that was built upon Genesis 3, where it reads:

> Then the man and his wife heard the sound of the Lord God as he was walking in the garden in the cool of the day, and they hid from the Lord God among the trees of the garden. But the Lord God called to the man, "Where are you?"
>
> He answered, "I heard you in the garden, and I was afraid because I was naked; so I hid."

He knew guilt was certainly the subject he wanted to talk about. Guilt was such a worthy topic to any congregation, and most any scripture could be bent in that direction, he thought with satisfaction. Yet, as he worked on his sermon with the Genesis text describing Adam and Eve's hiding from their shame for misbehavior, he sought an example that would amplify their guilt.

Pastor Quark had a habit of taking a little walk outside when he got stuck on sermon preparation. He went to his vegetable garden—not quite like he envisioned Eden being. For more authenticity, he wandered over to Mr. VanderBeek's apple orchard. There he could imagine Adam and Eve walking in the dewy morning, but it was hard to imagine the orchard being a very good hiding locale. In fact, it was a terrible place a person could try to hide; there was no cloaking vegetation until you came to the tree branches themselves, and they were a good four or five feet above the ground. As the good pastor ruminated upon this, he overheard some people talking and laughing. A couple of rows over, Bobby DeGlopper was telling some kid Pastor Quark didn't know about a Billy who had done a stupid thing just the day before.

Back in the office, Pastor Quark called Edna Harkness, knowing she would have the full story about what he had just overheard in the orchard. Edna affirmed the story and filled him in on the details.

The situation took place on an average day as eleven-year-old Billy Dennison was getting used to summer vacation. It started as Billy's big chance turned into a big fiasco. Both his parents worked and drove to and fro with the one car they owned. They would come home together at lunch and have a simple sandwich or a can of soup with Billy and his brother, Gary. Sometimes, Gary would be asked to have something simple ready for them, especially if his parents had another chore to handle during the lunch hour.

As Billy's mother was completing her list of chores for her boys to do that day, she also asked the most notable question of Billy's summer: "Would you like to cook our lunch today, Billy?"

To Billy, cooking was akin to magic. He had watched his mother take ingredients from the cupboard and refrigerator, mix them together, and cook them on the stove burners or bake the mixture in the oven with miraculous results. Dry spaghetti wasn't much to taste, and flour was pretty yucky. But throw in this, combine that, make some sauce in another pan, put them together, and you had this amazing tasty treat—Mom's mouth-watering Italian spaghetti.

Spaghetti was just one of the miracles his mother performed. Other marvels included stew, meatloaf, chicken and biscuits, scalloped potatoes and ham, and Billy's favorite: goulash. It wasn't just the taste but the smells, the textures, and the glorious visuals that got his stomach growling for chow. Billy had watched his mother and knew that the real secret of her culinary masterpieces came from the upper cabinet to the left of the stove. It was a treasure vault for little tin cans, little bottles, and some various-sized jars. It was when his mom reached in and poured tiny spoonfuls into the mix that the aromas got intense, a sure sign of flavors coming at the end. Like the ingredients in a magic potion, these powders, flakes, liquids, and leaves were the secrets of this enchanted art called cooking.

Would I like to cook lunch today? It was a dream come true. To be asked to be the chef of the Dennison lunch was an event, like getting your driver's license or going on your first date. Billy couldn't hide his eagerness as he repeated, "Yeah, yeah, yeah!"

Billy's mom said, "Okay then, come into the kitchen with me and I'll show you what you're going to do."

Billy followed his mother into the kitchen, where she opened a cabinet and removed a large can of Broadcast corned beef hash. Then she opened the lower oven drawer and removed a large black iron skillet. Setting that on the large front burner, she found the can opener and set it next to the can of hash.

"This is all you have to do," she said. "At about fifteen minutes before noon, put the hash on medium heat. Watch it, checking it every couple of minutes. When it's turned a little crusty brown, flip it all over and keep a watch on this side. When it gets lightly browned, turn the burner to low. We'll be home shortly, and we'll cook the eggs when we get here."

Billy nodded and said, "Okay. I got it."

"Quarter of twelve," his mother repeated. And then as a kind of verbal fine print, she added, "If you aren't sure, turn it down and wait till we get home."

The morning dragged by as Billy tried watching *Captain Kangaroo* and then the nine o'clock movie, where Laurel and Hardy were in the French Foreign Legion. He kept checking the mantel clock, which seemed to be barely moving. When the clock chimed for 11:30, Billy went to check the clock on the stove. This one read 11:33, and Billy was certain this electric clock was probably more accurate than the windup timepiece in the living room. He decided he might as well stay in the kitchen, being so close to "go" time.

At 11:38, Billy picked up the can opener, tested the grip, and opened and closed the handles. At 11:41, Billy pierced the can and twisted and removed the top. With a few minutes to go, Billy wondered if he should turn the stove on and get the burner hot, or was the 11:45 the time that he should actually turn on the heat? Wanting to be safe, Billy decided to turn the burner on, set the skillet on the burner, and wait with the opened can of hash hovering over the pan with a spoon ready to empty it as soon as the clock showed 11:45. The tension mounted and the excitement grew. The clock hands seemed to stop.

Finally at a quarter of twelve, the hash hit the hot pan with a sizzle. After scraping the can repeatedly to get every last morsel, Billy threw the can in the garbage and then stood staring at the moist hash nestled in the old skillet and expected to feel great waves of accomplishment. But he didn't.

This was not the magic that his mother used in the performance of cooking. What Billy had done was dump some stuff from one container to another. No busy moves between refrigerator and mixing bowl, no enchanted measuring cups filled and leveled, and especially no exotic substances out of the magic cabinet that conjured up aromas and flavors that appeared from an act of creative genius. This was scraping room-temperature bits of meat and potato into a hunk of iron in which he converted it into warmed bits of meat and potato. There had to be more. There would be more!

Billy might not need to select, prepare, and combine raw materials, but he could still do some magic. He reached for the upper cabinet to the left of the stove. His eyes searched the tin boxes, the cans, and the bottles, his hands hovering like the spirit over the chaos of cosmic stew on that first day of creation.

Many times Billy nearly took hold of a mysterious container, but uncertainty made him hesitate. He wasn't sure what this stuff would do. *Dill weed, garlic powder, anise, or lemon extract?* The fear of not knowing what aroma and taste would come from any of these additions froze Billy in uncertainty. He wanted to add an ingredient, but he was frightened of what taste he might create. Would vanilla enhance the hash? Would allspice improve corned beef? Would mace perk up tiny cubes of potato?

Billy felt defeated by the unknown consequences of ignorant seasoning. Then an inspiration struck like thunder on a still night.

There was a special category of magic in this cupboard that Billy's mother said, "It doesn't change the taste and it doesn't change the fragrance of the dish." It was almost too good to be true. A potion from this cabinet that could transform the food but not actually change the taste or the aroma? Astounding, yet true by his mom's own words.

With the daring of any hero, Billy reached for this remarkable substance. He opened the little box and gazed at the choices within. Billy reached in and took hold of destiny. He uncapped the small bottle and let the contents dribble into the hissing hash. A few stirs with a worn wooden spoon and the Broadcast corned beef hash took on a whole new dimension.

Billy suddenly had one of those serendipitous moments of truth. Beyond being his favorite color, he knew blue was a wonderful color for the sky, delightful for the ocean, and just fantastic for the eyes. But it was terrible—no, revolting—for hash!

Billy stared at this simple food that he had transformed into an ugly tub of corned beef *yuck*. There was no second chance at his choice, no second can of hash in the cupboard, and no second to spare. While his eyes took in the hideous concoction, his ears picked up the unmistakable crunching of gravel in the driveway. Billy's folks were home for lunch.

He ran upstairs, jumped on his bed, and covered his head with his pillow. His only desire was to hide. If there was any way he could avoid his mother or his father right now, he would give anything to be able to achieve it. To erase his choice and take back his decision was all he wanted at the moment.

Billy heard the squeak of the screen door, steps partway across the kitchen, and then a few seconds of nothing. He knew they had stopped in front of the stove. Billy pulled the pillow tighter. The steps continued, and the door to the stairs opened. The voice of his father said, "Billy. Billy! Where are you?"

> Then the man and his wife heard the sound of the Lord God as he was walking in the garden in the cool of the day, and they hid from the Lord God

> among the trees of the garden. But the Lord God called to the man, "Where are you?"

Billy slowly crawled from his bed, came to the head of the stairs, looked down at his father, and was surprised that his dad didn't look mad.

"I'm sorry," Billy began. Then the words tumbled out between gasps for air as tears formed. "My big chance and I ruined it! I'll never get to cook again."

> He answered, "I heard you in the garden, and I was afraid because I was naked; so I hid."

"Come on down here, little buddy," Billy's father said with a gentle tenor in his voice. "It's all right. You didn't ruin it. It's just food coloring. The hash hasn't changed taste." With a coaxing wave of his hand, his dad said, "Come on down. Let's eat." Billy climbed down the stairs, and his father put an arm around him as they walked together toward the dining room and the gourmet hash.

Pastor Quark took in this mishap of Billy Dennison, lined it up against his troubled text, and felt he really knew what that garden scene must have felt like for those two rascals in the garden who took such a wonderful opportunity and made blue hash out of it. He realized how poor decisions can alienate you from the people you need the most, and people find a way to hide from the confrontation, even if it is the only resolution available.

Quark also had a flash of insight with Billy's father's reaction. He could feel the compassion overruling the disappointment. The good pastor could sense how Billy's father had quickly moved past the error and concentrated on rebuilding the relationship.

Then he remembered where he was planning on taking this text—to guilt! Guilt was certainly involved, but the father didn't use it as a club, but as a useful setting from which to embrace his foolish son. But the fact was that Billy's father tried to go on as if nothing had happened, when Billy had made a mistake and the hash was blue!

Forgiveness of the mistake seemed good and even made Pastor Quark feel warm inside. But he could not buy the idea of everybody going to the table and eating that blasted blue hash! As he reflected upon the message he wanted to share with the congregation, he knew something was wrong or incomplete in all this. He believed in the forgiveness and tolerance, but mistakes were still mistakes—at least the result of the mistake remained.

He thought about Mrs. Filkins and her flare for gossip. Pastor Quark felt all right about forgiving her, but he wasn't about to make a meal of her rumormongering. And Mr. VanDyke and his foul language—well, that he could pardon. But he wasn't about to cover it up like nothing was wrong with it.

This made Pastor Quark wonder if everything was really that easily resolved in the Dennison home. He was partial to the scene in his mind's eye of Billy with his affectionate father's arm putting an end to that short-term estrangement, but something told him that could not really be the end of it.

Pastor Quark decided to pay the Dennisons a visit and play like Paul Harvey and learn "the rest of the story."

The next day, Pastor Quark saw Mr. Dennison outside the drugstore and asked if he had time to have a cup of coffee with him. He did, and they went inside and sat at the counter of Walgreens.

After some chitchat, Pastor Quark broached the subject of the blue hash.

"Oh, my goodness," Mr. Dennison said. "I never wanted to throttle a kid and laugh at the same time. You can't imagine what that goop looked like!"

"I'm sure I can't," Quark replied. "But just to feed my curiosity, what happened when you all got to the table? Did you really eat the blue hash?"

"I sure thought I could," Mr. Dennison said. "But when I scooped some hash onto my plate while everyone watched, I'll tell you. When that royal blue hash received my runny yellow egg, and then when I splashed on some red ketchup, I just about lost it."

"I can imagine. Please go on."

"Well, I dug my fork in, bravely stuck it in my mouth, tried to chew, but found a gagging reflex too much to overcome. I spit it out in the garbage and scrapped the rest of that blue hash with it!"

Pastor felt the truth of this incident but also wondered about how Billy took it. "Was Billy crushed that you really couldn't eat the hash?" In fact, it really proved that he *had* ruined it after all.

"I had the same fear, Pastor," Mr. Dennison said, staring off into that past moment. A flinch of sorrow was then replaced with a beaming smile. "I told Billy, who looked like he was going to cry. I told him that I thought I could eat it, but I couldn't in the end. But then I went to the cupboard, opened it, and found that we had another can of hash. So I told him, 'We'll just do it over. You can just do it over!' And he did."

Now that made sense, thought Quark.

And when he went back to working on that sermon, he realized that that was what God did with his disobedient children in the Garden of Eden. God didn't act like the apple had not been eaten, any more than we can declare an act of gossip not being uttered, or a foul word not escaping a mouth. God didn't ignore the sin; he sent Adam and Eve out of the garden.

But that was not the end of it. Mr. Dennison threw out the blue hash, and then they went at it fresh. Adam and Eve had to vacate the garden, but God gave them another chance. And finally it all led to Jesus, who took away real things. He didn't just pretend nothing was wrong, but erased real sin—and truly gave us a fresh start, once we've agreed it was the mistake it was.

Pastor Quark realized that you can overcome blue hash by opening a new can and starting again. And no matter how many times we make blue hash out of our lives, God is ready with that amazing grace and forgives and says, "Let's try it again!"

The Sunday Budget Meeting

Pastor Quark finished the reading of the scripture and hesitated, as if he was surprised that this was what today's text said. As he closed the heavy book, he repeated the words, "He who finds his life will lose it, he who loses his life will find it." With a little smirk and a knowing nod, he looked out at Bobby DeGlopper and the rest of the congregation through his oversized, dark-rimmed glasses (reminding Bobby of Hula-Hoops balanced on the nose of a very thin totem pole). "Yes, yes," Quark said, "finding and losing, losing and finding."

Doubtful that Pastor Quark would get much further than acting smug about the text's wonderful truth but never really letting the congregation in on just what that truth was, Bobby kneeled in the pew backward and got to the important task of staring at Mrs. Kubiac, who sat directly behind him. Bobby had always thought she was ornery and just pretended to be a good person. Now, as he watched her, she was probably just pretending to concentrate on the pastor's words, but she just didn't have the willpower. She would soon move her head in little nods to try and get Bobby to turn around in his seat. But he wouldn't; he would just smile a little. Soon Mrs. Kubiac would be gritting her teeth, blinking her eyes rapidly, and concentrating on her frustration. Bobby was sure that this was a better use of her time than tracking "the duck's" sermon.

Pastor Quark leaned forward to make his final appeal about "losing and finding." Then he raised his thin voice, even as he slowed the pace of his concluding words, and punched the big finish: "So let's all go out there and do it!"

Pastor Quark's right hand, which was holding onto the pulpit, at that next moment slipped. Bobby turned around to giggle at the silly sight of Pastor Quark nearly smashing his face into the large pulpit Bible. Then Bobby turned back to hand Mrs. Kubiac her hymnbook for the closing song: "Yield Not to Temptation." Apparently the temptation to which they were not yielding was to sing the hymn with some recognizable spirit and enthusiasm.

Bobby knew it was supposed to be an important day; more people than usual were here. It was called something like "Budget Shortfall Potluck Fund-Raiser" or those words in another order. Bobby had listened to his folks talk about this budget thing and knew that the church was in some sort of trouble.

The trouble came from the fact that Dr. White, who Bobby couldn't remember ever coming to church, had died a couple of years ago. He had always come to the deacons and given them a check for the "shortfall." The shortfall actually had nothing to do with falling or being physically short, but his dad had said they had more bills to pay than money to pay them with. Bobby reasoned that there was no more trouble than usual; they just didn't have Dr. White to bail them out. They should call this "Bailout Sunday," Bobby suggested once, but they didn't.

This potluck fund-raising affair became the church's answer. As Mr. Swattleberg said, "First you fill 'em up with food and then they have to loosen their belts, and so they might as well loosen their purse strings at the same time."

After benediction, people would normally get up casually and mosey toward the doors. Some stopped and chatted a bit before they left, while others browsed the table at the back of church to see if the new devotional was out for pickup. But today was a potluck day, and normal behavior made way for the hurried frenzy to get to the basement fellowship hall and get their place reserved.

Being a seasoned professional, Mrs. Kubiac deftly sliced her way to the back of the church well before young Bobby DeGlopper, who was well ahead of the frazzled Pastor Quark. When Mrs. Kubiac got to the back of the sanctuary, Bobby saw she was talking to Mr. Stienbrenen, the ancient vice chair of the board. She was talking rapidly, pointing his way, and gesturing with her head so violently that her hat—a large flowered affair—got twisted sideways and cocked a little over her right eye.

Now Bobby saw an opening in the crowd and was about to jump for the ledge that surrounded the stairwell, but just as he left his feet, a firm and weathered hand grabbed the back of his shirt collar. Bobby's eyes followed the hand up the arm to Mr. Stienbrenen's stern face. The old man bent almost in two so that his face was in Bobby's own.

"Listen, young man," Cal said, his temples visibly throbbing, "I've had it with you and your nonsense during the service!"

Bobby knew it was a good time to look scared and suitably intimidated by this forceful behavior of his senior.

"You should be listening to the preacher, not playing around. If this happens again I'm going straight to your mother to ask that she keep you out of the sanctuary!"

Did he really think this was a threat? Well, Bobby would act the part anyway. "Yes, sir. I'm sorry. I'll try to act better. I'm sorry!" Bobby had learned that uttering the word "sorry" was an essential part of getting off the hook. As Bobby did his best little gentleman walk down the stairs to the fellowship hall, he hoped that by chance his mom put their place settings across from Mrs. Kubiac.

Most everyone had found a place to sit, and after he clinked his glass for attention, Pastor Quark said a particularly long grace for the food. Immediately after his "amen," he attempted to offer some instructions for how people should proceed to the serving tables in order. But his words were covered by the noise of a general rush to the serving tables.

Bobby was desperately trying to fight the larger bodies to get into the line before the meat and lasagna were gone. All of a sudden he found his face in the back of Mrs. Kubiac, who was quick to inquire, "Where do you think you are going, hmm? Do you think you can play in church and not listen to the worship and still get to the front of the line?"

Bobby was sure that this all seemed quite logical to this humorless woman but somehow eluded any appearance of sense to him. But being used to dealing with the rationale of adults, he went along with it silently. Finally, he got his food, though the cheese on top of the lasagna was gone when he got to that station.

After the meal and while he was eating the frosting off the top of a second cupcake, the business of the budget began. The shortfall of this year's giving was presented by the treasurer, Mr. McIlroy. A $5700 deficit was received with a lot of gasping for breath. There was a movement, verbalized by Mrs. Kubiac, to explain this enormous deficit, that being the decision of some to replace the perfectly good wire hangers in the entryway that Louie's Dry Cleaners had donated with those expensive wooden ones. Though the cost of the wooden hangers was only $138, Bobby wondered how that explained the remaining $5500. After this mental exercise, Bobby gave up listening to the stupid discussion.

Apparently Bobby's mother was through listening at this time also, because she leaned over the table and spoke quietly to her son, whispering, "Bobby, I'm getting very tired of your behavior in church. And I'm tired of listening to Mrs. Kubiac and Mr. Stienbrenen tell me about it. Can't you just sit and listen to the message, and if not listen, just be quiet and let others listen?"

"But, Mom, I—" he started to protest, but she cut him off with a "Shush."

The budget discussion continued. Bobby tried listening again to an assortment of comments that seemed to being flying around the room, hoping to land as the perfect answer to the problem.

"We need another Dr. White to show up. We're attracting the wrong kind of folks!" This couldn't help the new people to feel real worthwhile, Bobby thought.

"Some people gotta start pullin' their weight around here. It can't continue to be fixed by the ones already givin' all the time!"

Cal Stienbrenen was the only one who stood up to talk, but Bobby figured Mr. Stienbrenen believed his words should be said from a bit higher position than the others. "Years back, we just took for granted that we had to pay our 10 percent. You just did it. But now people just pay what they got left over, and if they don't have much left after crazy spending, they don't give much. The pastor ought to be preaching tithing, and while he is at it, he should be preaching working on Sundays, wearing ties in church, and disciplining their children!"

Bobby saw that his mom blushed at this statement, and it did seem many eyes in the room had moved their way.

Someone caught a bit of Stienbrenen's words and supported the notion, saying, "Preacher, you should have spoken on giving today!"

"I thought he did," Bobby said to his mom a bit too loud for her comfort.

She replied with another "Shush!" and gave that mean look that always freaked Bobby out.

Pastor Quark tried to gain some order and overcome the general cacophony. "I could do a series on stewardship and its blessings—"

"He didn't even listen to his own sermon!" Bobby shouted at his mom.

This last outburst triggered a surprisingly agile Mrs. DeGlopper to grab Bobby's arm, head for the ladies' restroom, and give him the angry, wide-eyed, raised-eyebrow look all at one instant.

Bobby found himself up against the cold and sweating green bathroom wall. It had been a long time since he had been in the ladies' room. Maybe it was the time he put salt in the pastor's pulpit drinking water?

Bobby's mother's face had turned bright red, like the deficit, and half crazed. "You are driving me crazy, young man!" Her voice was agonized as she bit her lip. "You're the one acting up in church, and you're saying the other people aren't listening?"

"They aren't!" Bobby persisted. "Pastor Quark said that we in the church were to do things differently than other folks. We're supposed to 'loosen up' on what we want, and somehow that is supposed to make us find some better stuff!"

Bobby's mom concentrated and tilted her head a little as her little prophet continued.

"They're the ones that say I don't listen to the message, but they are the ones that won't loosen up in church. They are the ones that wouldn't lose their place getting out of church this morning.

Wouldn't lose their place in the food line at dinner. Mrs. Kubiac won't even let loose those stupid wooden hangers." Bobby kicked the stall door as to emphasize his words. "And I bet they all got money they could let loose but don't!" Bobby finished his argument with a sheepish expression and softer voice, saying, "I know I'm not always paying attention, Mom, but I can't say these other people find much of interest themselves."

"Why don't you stop looking at everyone else and just take care of yourself, Bobby," his mother said with an expression that puzzled him. She didn't look angry, more … something … what was it? Sorry? Then as if reading his thoughts, she said, "I feel bad for you, Bobby. All you can do is find fault with others! You never seem to examine your own actions or your own words. No. You just see what you can find wrong with everyone else." She was shaking her head slowly, and he knew this was something like pity.

With a last attempt to fight back, Bobby said, "But I listened better than they did!"

"Did you, Bobby?" Mrs. DeGlopper asked. "Did you really listen?"

"Yes!"

"What was the message today?"

"It was all about 'finding and losing, losing and finding,'" he said, parroting Pastor Quark with singsong mockery. "And they all need to lose some junk and—" He was cut off before he could finish.

Bobby's mother, with her finger to Bobby's lips, said, "Shush." Then she dropped her hand to his shoulder and spoke quietly. "Bobby, you are just judging others, when you first ought to look at yourself. Pastor did talk about losing and finding today. And you should *lose* your attitude and *find* some humility."

Bobby was quiet.

"What have *you* been willing to lose today? What have *you* found this morning?" A smile played at the edge of his mother's mouth. "Do you understand what I'm saying?"

Bobby got the drift and did his own losing and finding. He *lost* his television privileges for a week, and two weeks' allowance that he was "encouraged" to drop in the Budget Recovery Offering. And he *found*, to his surprise, that his mom might be right. He was harder on others than he was on himself.

Again, he considered Pastor Quark's scripture for the day: "He who finds his life will lose it, and he who loses his life for my sake will find it." Bobby also *found* that this scripture stuff was meant for him, not just others, and it wasn't nearly as much fun this way.

The Music School of Hard Knocks

On a hot August-like September day, the grass was brown, and the dark green swing seats and teeter-totter boards were hotter than the burning sands of the playground. Mrs. VanHuizen—the playground lady at DeGroote Street School—wandered the recreational dunes, like a camel on her eighth day without water. Her slow, deliberate gum chewing and her bristled chin did little to refute that picture.

The first bell clanged and the kids lined up by the doors to go into the school. Mrs. VanHuizen made it to the door just in time for the second bell and, through her panting for breath, told the last two stragglers to get in line and not to run. This was way before elementary kids had to go through metal detectors and get frisked by uniformed guards. The kids streamed into the dim hall of the fourth- and fifth-grade wing.

"Kid stuff!" Butch Carson said as he stood by the second-floor window that overlooked the playground below.

This scene exposed what an amazing difference a couple of years make and how mature and sophisticated one becomes in a few hundred days. Not only was Butch no longer a little kid taking part in recess, but he had more grown-up things to think about. He and his classmates' social life did not end with the final school bell on Friday.

Now as mature seventh graders at Potowasso Junior High, Butch and his friends were anticipating their first dance. Friday night at seven o'clock, the doors to the gymnasium would open, and he and his buddies would be transported to official teenage heaven—a dance with records and girls and everything!

Butch never thought much about intolerance before, but he would learn it was all around at his first school dance. Music had always seemed so safe to Butch, but he was going to learn that music and its culture proved to be as dividing as team colors, politics, or religion.

Butch had heard and liked the idea that music was the universal language. It made him think of different-colored kids walking arm in arm around the UN building all smiles, because some simple tune bound them together like brothers and sisters on Walton's Mountain. But the language of prejudice seemed pretty widespread also.

Being a man of the world, Butch had made a date for the big dance—a real date with LuEllen Lavellier. They were going to have one of those nights that dreams were made of. LuEllen promised to meet him at the punch bowl at the first signs of the DJ putting "Blue Velvet" on the turntable. And after the dance they would meet up and go for fries and a Coke at Fanny's Cafe.

A date was a complicated concept, especially in junior high. A young man, like Butch, could be considered to be "going out" or "on a date" by the strange start of actually traveling to the dance with his buddies and simply meeting a girl sometime that evening for the briefest of times, as was the plan of Butch, who traveled to the dance, not with his date but with his friends, Jonathan and Runt VanDis.

After students were released from school on Friday afternoon, it was a dizzying time of trying on everything in their closet. Butch finally decided on his white shirt, striped tie, and his only sports jacket. It was a dark wool jacket with a herringbone pattern of dark chocolate and a muddy tan. But when he got to Jonathan's house, he was overwhelmed, in awe, and embarrassed all at once. English music groups were invading the country, even making headway into Potowasso, which seemed to still be holding tight to the wholesome 1950s. The Beatles had made their appearance on Ed Sullivan and never left most young people's minds and imaginations after that. They didn't do much for Butch, but he kept that to himself, so as not to be considered "square."

Runt, who was one of the shortest kids Butch knew, was nevertheless Jonathan's older brother. He had been held back a year and therefore was still in their grade. He answered the door wearing a really nice navy-blue blazer with a crest, gray slacks, paisley tie, and wing tips shining like wet Tootsie Pops. Runt looked older and kind of like a playboy in Munchkinland.

Butch made a quick assessment of his duds and was overcome with feelings of inadequacy. But that was a comparatively good feeling as he watched Jonathan come out of the bedroom. It was as if Paul McCartney lived here and Butch was just finding out.

"Twist and Shout" was blaring on the hi-fi, and Burrhead went into a twisting, arching, bucking flurry. What he was wearing, though, must have been his mother's original creation: an avocado-green suit of tight-pegged pants, no lapels or collar on the jacket, only dark green piping around the edges. He was a Beatle. Now his own Sunday school sports coat felt like something out of a museum, an out-of-touch, *ugly* clothes museum.

Jonathan was grinding his feet into the carpet while his arms and upper body seemed to be in some apoplectic gyration in the opposite direction. He feared that somewhere near Jonathan's waist, his body might break in two, like an overused twist tie. And that was when he noticed the hair.

Jonathan had been letting his hair grow since the Beatle bug bit him. Until now, as it had gotten longer, it didn't seem cool but more like a hundred other kids who had gone a long time without a trip to Mario's Barber Shop. Without these hip clothes, Jonathan had just looked shaggy and maybe a little poor. But when that long hair—nearly touching his collar and settling just over the top half of his ears—was crowning that body that wore the spiffy Beatle jacket and Beatle tight slacks, then suddenly Jonathan became a with-it visitor from Liverpool. It made Butch expect to hear Ed Sullivan's voice saying, "Now, on our stage, all the way from England, Jonathan McCartney!"

Butch knew right then that he had to rush home and check his closet again. Maybe he had some Beatle clothes that he had forgotten about. Or at least he could change into clothes that would somehow make his appearance a bit more newfangled and groovy.

Butch said, "Gotta go home a minute!" He turned to sprint for the door, running right into Moose.

Moose VanDis was Jonathan and Runt's dad. Moose was rather large—tall and thick, and his hands looked like hams on the ends of massive arms. He wore black engineer boots about the size of submarines, like-new starchy blue denim pants, and a navy-blue sweatshirt that had ridden up to expose his imposing belly with a belly button like a Florida sinkhole. He had little pig eyes, red from a short trip to the Veterans of Foreign War post with the boys after his day at the paper mill. Moose's hair was short, greased, and parted with a straightedge.

Moose stared at Jonathan and said, "You ain't leavin' this house with that hair!" Then after a pause for inspection, he added, "What in the heck is that you got on?" Moose had been complaining about Jonathan's ever-lengthening hair and odd clothing all summer.

"But, Dad—" Jonathan tried.

"I don't wanna hear it!" Moose bellowed. "You look like a sissy!"

Butch said, "Nice to see you, Mr. VanDis. Guess I'll be going now." He pushed through the screen door, jumped off the front stoop, and ran across the street and through the vacant lot. He stepped on the bent fence and raced to his back door. He couldn't help but feel he had just run out on a friend, but what was he to do really? Moose was Jonathan's dad, not his. And Moose was MOOSE! That was scary enough to chase John Wayne away.

Butch did his best to forget his buddy and the confrontation he was having with his dad, but he suddenly had a vision of Moose prohibiting Jonathan from attending the dance. Butch's solace was his steady faith in Jonathan to be sly enough to overcome any barrier Moose would try to set to keep Beatle boy from reaching his destiny at the school dance. The god of teen coolness would not let a miracle outfit like that go to waste. Jonathan was not destined only to go to the Potowasso Junior High dance, but to be the big attraction. The little backwater town of Potowasso in the dull Midwest needed a fashion hero, and Jonathan was clearly it!

The kids of Potowasso needed a revolutionary to free them from their humdrum, dreary style captivity. If someone didn't rise up and break the constrictive hair code, they could get stuck with neat hair the rest of their lives. Those with big ears, as Butch saw himself, would never know the comfort of the veil of hair, the mantilla of mane, or the cloak of their own locks. They would be unable to cover forehead blemishes and eventually their eyes. If Jonathan was somehow sidetracked from making it to the dance tonight, all boys in Potowasso could be sentenced to a lifetime of being clean-cut.

Butch rejected any thoughts of Jonathan not being able to attend and ran upstairs to rifle through his closet for some better clothes to wear to the big dance. He found a shirt that might just be a fashion rescue and yelled, "Aha!" It was what they called at the time "surfer shirts." They weren't Hawaiian prints but rather solid-colored, three-button, collarless shirts with contrasting colored piping around the neck and at the end of the short sleeves. Butch's was navy blue with white piping.

He slipped his surfer shirt on, rolled the lapels of his jacket inside, stuck a couple of safety pins to peg his pants and, voilà, he was a Beatle too!

Butch heard the horn outside and hustled down the stairs and out the door. To his relief, Jonathan was there with his brother, Runt, in their older sister Judy's red Corvair convertible.

"Hey! Cool!" Jonathan shouted genuinely when he saw his amazing attire. Jonathan's older sister, Judy, just said, "Oh boy!" and seemed to be stifling a laugh. Butch felt like a member of a cool guys club, going to the coolest event in their lives to listen to cool music, in really cool clothes.

When they arrived at the gymnasium entrance, where the dance was being held, they rushed in all excited. Butch was trying to control himself; he wanted to gawk in wide-eyed amazement and holler in excitement, and he wanted to look cool, which meant *not* looking excited about the sights and sounds. But apparently he was not controlling his outward excitement so well.

"First time out of the nest, Butch?" Lloyd, an eighth-grade jerk, said and laughed with a few of his buddies. "Yeah," he said, stroking his chin like Pa Kettle, "I remember my first dance. I hope I didn't look that stupid." And his buddies quickly picked up the cue and laughed some more.

Butch walked away, trying to will the redness out of his cheeks that he knew must be there. He made more of an effort to look casual and indifferent and, therefore, cool. As he wandered around the fringe of the gymnasium, he was struck by the kids in the middle of the floor. There were mostly boys and girls paired up but a few purely girl duos dancing. He watched a moment and saw different kids he knew looking quite at home on the ole dance floor. *Where did they learn that stuff?* Butch thought to himself.

He knew that he and LuEllen were going to meet as "Blue Velvet" began, but somehow he'd avoided the next step in logic—that he would then *dance* with her. He didn't know how to dance. It now dawned on him as quite odd that going to a dance was more about a social scene than the physical action from which it got its name. He went to a dance, but he hadn't thought about actually dancing so much. He hoped they played a slow song before "Blue Velvet" so he could see what a slow dance was supposed to look like.

Butch calmed down from being too excited about the atmosphere or too nervous about having to actually dance and just watched everyone talking, laughing, checking out each other's fashions, and trying not to give the impression of being nervous talking to someone of the opposite sex. He finally got beyond looking and began listening.

To be honest with himself, he was a bit let down as the music rolled on. He knew these songs were right off the charts: "Downtown" (Petula Clark), "You've Lost That Lovin' Feelin'" (The Righteous Brothers), "This Diamond Ring" (Gary Lewis & the Playboys), "Stop! in the Name of Love" (the Supremes), and of course "Eight Days a Week," "Help!" "Yesterday," and "Ticket to Ride" (the Beatles). But that was not the same as being familiar around Potowasso.

In the early and mid-sixties, his folks, like everybody else's folks, still controlled most of the radios at home. The kids may have been ready to move on to the new stuff that would eventually define their generation, but their ears were used to other things.

Butch was standing next to Runt and said, "Isn't this great!" when Sonny and Cher sang "I Got You Babe," but his heart was actually longing for Eddie Arnold's "What's He doing in My World," Patsy Cline's "Crazy," and Chet Atkins's reworked Boots Randolph's tune "Yakety Sax" as "Yakety Axe." He held back his real question: *Where was Conway Twitty and Loretta Lynn?*

Butch had friends within an enclave of transplants from the hills of Kentucky and Tennessee, who lived in the highland west of Potowasso. He knew what they listened to and couldn't help but imagine that the few of them he saw at the dance tonight had ears tuned to yet other sounds. He wondered if they were pretending to like this new teen music, while their hearts longed to hear Bill Monroe, Carter Stanley, Vassar Clements, Flatt and Scruggs, Reno and Smiley, Jim and Jesse McReynolds, and Ralph Rinzler. As he was asking where Conway and Loretta were, were they wondering where the Bluegrass Boys, the Greenbriar Boys, and a number of other colors of boys were? They all would probably make the shift to rock music, but it was harder than anybody wanted to let on.

Butch checked out the punch bowl, found Jonathan dipping into the red liquid, and asked him, "How did you get your dad to let you come to the dance? I thought he was going to stop you."

Jonathan told him that it was simply a matter of being quicker to the back door than Moose. In fact, as they rode away from the house, Moose was in the street, shrieking curses and promising great retribution when Jonathan got home.

Jonathan changed the subject and asked Butch, "Don't you love this music? Isn't it the coolest stuff you ever heard?"

Butch played along and said, "Yeah! This is really cool. I could listen to it all night."

Finally, "Blue Velvet" flowed from the speakers and LuEllen was suddenly right in front of him, eyebrows arched in some sort of beckoning expression. Butch had a great urge to run the other way. He nearly was in a panic as he thought about all these alien experiences happening all at once—this strange music, being expected to dance, and actually touching a girl's hands as they finally connected on this first real date.

Butch had watched a slow dance and couldn't see that they were doing much more than wobbling from one foot to the other, while they slowly rotated around the room and on their own axis. He tried to convert it into a geometry formula and just follow the formula. It didn't always work, because sometimes he and LuEllen went in opposite directions, only staying together because of a firm handhold. Then there were times that they collided or Butch stepped squarely on her foot. This dancing could make you crazy. It was wonderful to actually be touching and this close for this long, but it was terrifying to try and coordinate this attempt to move as a team.

The last dance of the evening was called, and the DJ played "Hey Paula." Butch danced with LuEllen, no longer frightened to dance; it was now just a little unnerving. They got their coats and walked down the two dim blocks to downtown and found a booth at Fanny's. Over a shared order of French fries, they talked, and Butch was beginning to feel somewhat at ease with LuEllen. They had a number of things in common, and both had cats as pets. They began to recap their experiences from their first dance.

LuEllen said, "I just love Leslie Gore. Don't you?"

Before Butch could answer, she added, "And aren't the Kingsmen and 'Louie, Louie' just the best?"

Butch had mistaken comfort for similarity of taste. "They're okay," he said. "But don't you miss Patsy Cline and Eddie Arnold?"

LuEllen stared blankly at Butch, who believed she wanted him to say more about this.

"And how on earth," Butch obliged, "do you play current music without ever playing 'The End of the World' by Skeeter Davis? Am I right?"

"What on earth are you talking about?" LuEllen asked. "It sounds like you like country and western music!"

"Well, yeah. Don't you like—"

"I think country music is stupid," LuEllen spit at him. "Are you kidding me? You're not, are you!" This last statement came out like an accusation of disgust.

Butch tried to backtrack, sensing his mistake. "I just mean I hear it a lot, and my folks and their friends like it."

LuEllen interrupted him. "You do like country music." Then she squinted like she just realized what an ugly creature she was confronting.

Finally, Butch got his dander up and blurted out, "Yes! I like my country and western music."

At this, LuEllen got up, grabbed her coat, and walked out of the diner. Butch was at a loss as to what to do. So he just sat there and watched LuEllen out on the sidewalk until her parents' car pulled up and she jumped inside and they sped away.

Butch was paralyzed, wondering what had just happened. He finally got up, paid the check, and slowly walked home, replaying the whole evening like a movie whose ending he didn't understand.

The next day, Butch heard the voices at the vacant lot next to the Blessing house and knew that the guys were gathering to play football. He snatched his red football helmet, ran through his backyard, hopped the wire fence, using it like a springboard, and bounded into the field of play.

Only three of the eight or so guys had helmets; one of them was Jonathan. At the end of the game, Butch's team winning by a trick play touchdown, they lingered to catch their breath and taunt the losers with clever remarks, like "You girls might want to practice a little more before you play against the men next time!" and "Maybe your barrettes were too tight!"

As they laughed and kept up the banter, Jonathan pulled his helmet off, and everyone went silent. Al his long hair was gone, and just fuzz and some angry gouges on his scalp were all that was left.

"What happened to you?" a number of boys asked at once.

Jonathan recounted last night after the dance.

Apparently his dad, Moose, was big and slow but patient. He sat in the living room with the lights off, watching an old western on TV. When Jonathan and Runt got home, Moose seemed to have cooled down. He nodded and grunted as the boys headed for their bedrooms.

"Night, Dad," they said and headed for their room.

"Good night, boys," Moose said rather congenially, which Jonathan thought was a good sign, so he was able to get to sleep without much trouble. And Jonathan slept deeply.

He never heard his bedroom door open. He never sensed Moose standing over him. He didn't even feel the compression of the bed until he felt his arms constricted by his dad's knees constricting them. He awoke to find Moose straddling him with his enormous bulk. Then Jonathan saw and heard the electric hair trimmer in the shadows of his room. A few minutes of screams and wild bucking and it was over.

"I'll show you a rock-and-roll haircut, you little sissy!" Moose said. "Here, I'll just 'twist' the hair, and you can just 'shout,' you little mop head!"

Jonathan lost his long hair, sheared like a sheep by a man named Moose. Jonathan might have listened to, and even loved, the Beatles, but it would be a long time until he looked like one again. And Butch could sense that he had lost the energy that his friend usually exhibited. He was noticeably humiliated as he told his story. And he was shocked at his dad's reaction to a few inches of hair that he blamed on the music Jonathan listened to.

Jonathan had lost the identity that his hair had brought him, but sadly he received a new identity with a new name: "Burrhead." Some clever and observant soul had said he looked like a sand burr that first day in school after the dance, and it stuck.

Butch felt bad for Burrhead and also for all his classmates for the setback that Jonathan's shearing represented. Somehow hair length and the new music were coupled like peanut butter and jelly, like rock and roll, like sand burrs and summer. Simply playing and appreciating that new music created such a horrible outcome for Burrhead, a nickname he would never shed.

As he examined Jonathan's shaved head from the back row in history class, and then looking across the room to where LuEllen was doing her best to ignore him in class, just like she had in the hallway whenever their paths crossed, Butch realized the irony of it all. His buddy got his head shaved because he liked rock-and-roll music, and he got dumped by a girl because he liked country and western songs.

Butch was getting another education about the world he lived in, this time through the music school of hard knocks in Potowasso.

The Big Scoop

With school back in session and the grace and beauty of fall creeping into the plans and activities, Potowasso became a bustling community. The merchants were sweeping the sidewalks daily, ready for the various hunting seasons to fire off. The city crews would be vacuuming leaves soon. The sight of trailers hustling firewood around town was common and the consequential smoke would soon be curling from every chimney.

More than smoke was in the air on those Friday nights; a glow in the western sky would mean that a football game was being played at Wooden Shoe Stadium. The sky would also come alive with assorted ducks, Canadian geese, and the swoosh of the haunting wings of Snow Geese, all en route to a winter destination. Part of the sky travelers would also be the Red-winged Blackbirds, which would become the trigger to a series of educational events in Billy Dennison's life one fall.

As the days shortened and cooled, the people in Potowasso were busy with seasonal rituals, much like the birds. Esau Kaiser was wearing red long johns that showed from his rolled-up shirtsleeves. Widow VanVliek had her wool, plaid scarf tied so tight that she had trouble speaking, her jaw being in the grip of a square knot. Mr. Gleeder, the grocer, was sorting pumpkins by size under the awning in front of his store. And Howard Avery was burning the midnight oil at the *Potowasso Union*, the local weekly newspaper.

The *Potowasso Union*—called the "Onion" by locals—bulked up in the fall: more activities to announce, more sales to advertise, and more accidents to report. Mr. Avery, who always seemed loaded with projects and deadlines, became an even busier editor, publisher, reporter, and typesetter from September through December.

The *Union* was located kitty-corner from the library and next to the alley that led to the Elks Lodge. It was a beige-painted brick building, with huge windows nearly floor to ceiling. The word "UNION" was engraved in the granite cornerstone. Above the front door lintel was a milky-white pane of glass with black fading Bookman Old Style numerals—"106." The large front windows didn't look like they had been washed in the last few years, and a sheet of sunbaked, brittle, translucent green plastic was stretched and taped across the top two feet of the windows, in an attempt to protect Mr. Avery from the afternoon sun.

Howard Avery sat at his big oak aircraft carrier-sized desk, behind piles of papers, books, and assorted tokens of life in Potowasso. Two large ashtrays were positioned at either end of the massive desk, overflowing with crunched cigarette butts and piles of gray ash. One was stationed by his typewriter on his right, and the other ashtray was positioned near a two-drawer file cabinet, which doubled as a coffee bar.

An ever-present cloud of smoke and steam surrounded Mr. Avery as he worked at his desk. He never touched his Pall Mall with his hands once he lit it. The tobacco burned down, and the ash grew to a length that spurned gravity as it rested in Avery's bouncing lips. He slouched in his worn swivel chair, the phone stuck between shoulder and cheek, while he typed on his old Royal. He was taking a quote from Luella Strombert at the Methodist church about this year's annual Harvest Bazaar. A clump of ash fell on his pinstriped wool pants without notice, and it made a person wonder why there was any ash in the ashtray.

There was nothing out of the ordinary about the *Union*. It was like most weeklies in the nation: lots of advertisements next to local reports, like the "Fishing Report," the "Church News," the "School Board Minutes," and the "Police Report," filled with misdemeanors. The format and features were usual, but one thing set the little paper apart—the caustic and inventive editorials that Howard Avery concocted and printed weekly. The rest of the paper could be written and reported by Joe Blow, but the editorial was like a James Thurber short story. Avery was witty, sarcastic, and unabashed. Once he wrote a column about Mayor DeLoof's proclivity toward "Cadillacs on a Ford Fairlane Salary." He once said that fourth district congressional representative Gerald Ford had blocked one too many linebackers. He referred to local state representative, Dickey Martin, as "the dandy with dimples, but short on brains." He called Lyndon Johnson a "power-hungry Texan who never saw a sick policy that he couldn't bribe back into health." And he called the ERA an attempt by women to justify their inability to cook a decent meal.

To say that Howard Avery was outspoken was to describe the Willis Towers as "rather tall." Howard Avery was a rebel, a dissident, a malefactor, and a really funny guy. Most folks didn't know if it was respect or fear they should have for Avery, but they certainly dreaded the day he would discover the peccadillo in their lives. Potowasso seemed to hold its collective breath, waiting to see what Avery's column would uncover this week. No one seemed safe and out of his reach. Becoming the "big scoop" of the week, a person's only salvation from public embarrassment was next week's scoop that would leave last week's story in the dust.

Billy Dennison was the fifteen-year-old son of Mort Dennison, a foreman at the paper mill. Billy liked to read anything he could get his hands on, and though he didn't understand Howard Avery's editorials all the time, he still thought they were the greatest thing since Cracker Jack. Billy was somewhat shy and did nothing outstanding that brought him even a whiff of fame. The notoriety of Mr. Avery was probably what attracted Billy so much. People knew the newspaperman was around and they were careful of him. Howard Avery had people compliment him to his face and shiver in apprehension behind his back. Billy wanted to be just like that, which is why he wanted to work with him or for him or—more to the point—be him! He craved that kind of attention and dreamed about the fame Avery must enjoy. *Oh, to get the big scoop on someone!*

Billy had toyed with the idea of getting a job at the paper but figured it would have to wait until he got older. That's why it surprised even Billy when he veered off the sidewalk and through the door of the *Union*. He choked on the stale smoke filling the air, squinted through the haze, and found himself standing before his legend Howard Avery's desk. He was at his typewriter, mumbling around a burning cigarette, as he struck the keys and slapped at the return lever. Suddenly his typing halted, along with the mumbling, and he looked with bloodshot eyes over heavy, black-rimmed glasses. Avery glared at him, as if he was some visible virus attempting to infiltrate his respiratory system. He had gray, wavy, uncontrollable hair and wrinkled skin. He waited in silence, staring a hole through the frozen Billy.

"Pardon me," Billy finally squeaked. "Mr. Avery ... sir ... I ... I ... am Bill Dennison, Mort and Dolly's son. I was wondering ... was hoping ... thinking ... dreaming ... that maybe I could do some writing for the paper ... your paper!" Then Billy swallowed and was sure that it could be heard in the next county.

Howard Avery just kept staring, like he didn't believe what had slithered into his office, his throne room.

"Mr. Avery," Billy stuttered, "is it possible to ... is it thinkable to ... for me to write something for you and the *Union*?" He felt like he was asking the pope if he would mind if he wrote his next encyclical.

An inch and a half of cigarette ash dropped to the floor. The second hand on the wall clock thundered to the next second. And his head tilted back so he could look through his glasses at the bug before him. Then a whole lot of pause ... delay ... scrutiny. Finally, he swiveled in his chair, threw a half-sheet of white paper in the carriage of the Royal, pecked a coupled of lines, and with a flick of the wrist, the half-sheet kicked out and into his waiting nicotine-yellowed fingers.

"Here," Avery growled, handing the paper to Billy. "Mrs. Althea Rosequist. Taught school about a hundred years. Still does some tutoring or something. Been doing it for about fifty years. She's about two hundred years old and still tickin'. She'd make a good byline."

Billy looked at the paper and saw Mrs. Rosequist's name and an address. A couple of spaces below that was the phrase

"Blackbirds in Sherman Woods." As if reading my mind, Howard Avery supplemented his typed words by saying, "This time of year blackbirds flock down in the woods. Find out why and get a couple of pictures—black-and-white photographs. Give you a byline on that too." Then he turned around and went back to his smoking and typing and mumbling.

Wow! Billy had two assignments from Howard Avery. Maybe not the big scoop assignments, but they were byline assignments—whatever that was. Billy ran to the five-and-ten, bought a spiral notepad and a new Paper Mate pen, and told the clerk it was for his new assignment at the *Union*. Then he rode his bike down a few blocks to the address on the piece of paper Mr. Avery had given him. He leaned his bike against a large maple tree in the front yard, jumped up on the porch, and rang the doorbell.

A really nice-looking lady, about Billy's grandmother's age, he guessed, came to the door.

"May I help you?" she asked.

"I'm ..." Who was he? A reporter? A writer? Should he say he worked for the paper? Could he say he worked for the paper? "I'm Billy Dennison, Mort and Dolly's son." When you've got names to drop, why try anything else? He told this lady that he wanted to write an article about her.

And after a brief explanation of his reporting errand for the *Union*, this lady told him that she was Mrs. Rosequist's granddaughter. Billy was dumbfounded by this revelation. Maybe a hundred was lowballing Mrs. Rosequist's age after all.

"I'm sorry," Billy said. "I thought you might be...." But he stopped that train of thought as he noticed this lady before him squinting like his mother did when he asked her if they had radios when she was a kid. "Could I see your grandmother?"

She thought that the idea was nice, but he would have to come back next week when hopefully her grandmother would be feeling stronger.

What a letdown. Wait a whole week to get his big scoop?

Billy looked at the half sheet of paper from Mr. Avery's office and read, "Blackbirds in Sherman Woods." He figured all the birds would be healthy but doubted any of them would give him an interview. And he frankly didn't know what else to do. To write an article, he had figured on going somewhere and asking some questions, kind of writing the conversation down, and that's what would go in the paper.

But this bird thing had him stumped. He'd have to figure out what to write later; for now he'd settle for some sort of picture. He'd go get his Brownie camera and take some pictures of the woods and the blackbirds.

Sherman Woods was a large stand of maples that began at the end of Sherman Road, just beyond the new housing development, Shady Grove Acres. Billy knew the place well; his aunt and uncle had one of the very first houses built there. They had a creek behind their house, and his cousin Martha and he would follow it all the way back to Sherman Woods, even as far back as the old abandoned Sherman place.

Howard Avery lived across the street from Uncle Bob. That was probably why he knew about the blackbirds in the woods there, Billy reasoned.

He leaned his bicycle against the outdoor lamp pole, grabbed his camera, and knocked on the back door. Martha answered the door. Billy exploded with all the great news about working for Mr. Avery. And when he told her about his chance to get a byline, she said she didn't know what that was.

"Is Uncle Bob home?" Billy asked her, after he ran out of things to say about his encounter with her neighbor, the editor.

"No. He and Mom went to town for something," his cousin said. "I'm not supposed to say anything about what they're doing."

Billy waited. He knew Martha. He knew how poorly she could keep a secret. She'd blabbed enough of the ones he had told her. His silence was as good as Chinese water torture on Martha.

"Really," she squealed. "I can't talk about it!"

Billy rolled his tongue around the inside of his mouth and let his eyes roam around the ceiling.

"Okay! Okay! I'll tell you. But you've got to promise not to say anything to anybody, Billy. Okay?"

Billy nodded his head, knowing that as long as he avoided giving his actual word (out loud) it wasn't really binding somehow. Heck, he was a reporter anyway, always on the trail for news—not to keep promises!

"Dad went to borrow some tools and stuff so he can knock out the basement wall." Martha giggled and added, "He's gonna do it in the middle of the night."

"Why?" Billy asked, clueless to what this could be about but beginning to smell a story.

"You know the sailboat he built?"

Martha's dad had been in the navy, and whether or not that was the reason, it seemed logical; he liked to sail. He had built a little sailboat that a couple of people could sit on and skim over Pine Lake. Billy had done it with him and found it great fun. But his Uncle Bob also liked to build things. For two years he had been building a much bigger sailboat in his basement—on his workshop side, where Billy and Martha hadn't been able to play since the project began. They had found it interesting to see it take shape. They often watched him from the doorway as he sanded the wood or cut pieces with his saw.

Like most everyone else, Billy had asked, "How are you going to get this big boat out of the basement?" And Uncle Bob had always confidently said, "Believe it or not, it will just fit up the stairway and right out the back door at the top of the stairs." He was sure because he had measured and calculated the size of the boat using the plans he had gotten from *Popular Mechanics*. He was following these plans precisely, and the boat would "slip up the stairs like a shadow."

"The sailboat he built is finished." Martha laughed as she said it. "He tried to get it upstairs last night. It wouldn't fit!"

"You're kidding!" Billy said. "So Uncle Bob is going to have to take out a basement wall to get it out?"

"Yeah! He's gonna try tonight. Real late tonight." Martha's eyes were nearly as big as her mouth.

"But why in the middle of the night?" Billy asked. But even before the last word was out of his mouth, he knew. Howard Avery lived across the street, and Uncle Bob was scared that this giant mistake would be on the front page of the *Union*. Uncle Bob was worried that he would be the biggest joke in Potowasso since Police Chief Grevenstuk backed over the city hall flagpole on the Fourth of July (and it was rumored that it was more than just the sky that was lit up that night).

"So you can't tell Mr. Avery or anybody," Martha pleaded. "Okay?"

Billy quickly crossed his fingers behind his back, effectively removing any burden of truth-telling right then. "Okay," he said and nodded. "I won't tell Mr. Avery a thing."

The phone rang, and Martha was too busy making someone else swear to secrecy to notice Billy sneaking down the stairs to take a couple of snapshots of the beautiful boat in front of the soon-to-be-removed cement block wall.

Uncle Bob was able to dig out the basement wall, remove the blocks, and scoot the sailboat to the backyard under a tarp. It took a week, but he had cleverly spread the news of putting in a new sump pump. He believed, and was therefore relieved, that he was safe from the truth about his night adventure getting into the wrong hands. He never suspected his nephew, Billy. He never knew that Billy had brought his camera in the daytime and took several snapshots of the pile of dirt and the hole in the basement wall.

Cousin Martha told Billy that her dad was relieved "big time" that he had gotten away with it, especially with Mr. Avery right across the street. Billy was busting inside to tell Martha what he had done and what he was going to do with it. Billy headed straight downtown to the *Union* to turn in his big scoop with the black-and-white photographs.

This would certainly get him a byline (whatever that was) and get his name in the paper as well. He was a real reporter, one of those investigative reporters who get the secret story of clandestine affairs and covert activities. He was like a secret agent with a ballpoint pen instead of a Beretta. Someday he would expose white-collar crime and maybe even presidential misbehaviors. Whatever the case, he knew he had real promise in this business.

Billy couldn't wait to see Howard Avery's face when he handed in his story and the accompanying photos. *Boy, will Mr. Avery be impressed. He thought I was just a little kid. I guess this will dazzle him.* There were a couple of clever lines, a few slick phases Billy had come up with of which he was particularly proud. It was a dream come true to have a great writer like Howard Avery praise his work!

Billy was as sure as he could be that praise was about to fall all over him. Mr. Avery would probably write an article in the paper about what a good writer and investigative reporter Billy was. It might hit the wires—the Associated Press might send it all over the country, all over the world! Well, in a moment of caution Billy thought perhaps he should just see if Avery would publish it in the *Potowasso Onion* before he celebrated his newfound worldwide fame.

Billy jumped off his bike before it stopped, vaulted into the *Union*, and slammed his story on Mr. Avery's desk. A long ash fell from the publisher's cigarette as he turned and stared at the photos and the written report lying before him. He didn't smile. He didn't seem surprised. He slowly took his smoke and crushed it in the ashtray.

"This is your uncle, isn't it? Bob is your mother's brother?"

"Yep!" Billy replied eagerly.

"He doesn't know you took these pictures or wrote this story." He said it as a statement, not a question. "You want to run with this? You sure you want to run with this?" He looked at Billy over those heavy glasses of his. One eye seemed to twitch a little.

"Yes," Billy said. "I sure do! And maybe a byline too?"

"Oh," he said, "I wouldn't do this without a byline." He dropped Billy's story on an overflowing basket of papers. "We'll see," he said, and Billy knew that that was the end of the conversation.

Attempting a confident stride, Billy walked out to his bike and rode off into his new life of fame and fortune. He waited three days before the *Potowasso Union* hit the newsstands. When it did, he was the first customer at Colburn's Drugstore. When he approached the stack of papers on the bottom shelf of the magazine rack, he could see one of his photographs. He had made the front page, above the fold—incredible.

Billy slapped his dime on the counter and ran into the alley behind Colburn's to bask in the glow of celebrity. The picture had come out very well. It was the one of the sailboat before the basement wall had been dismantled. And in inch-tall letters next to the picture was the headline: "BOB DAVIS FINISHES TWO-YEAR PROJECT." Underneath were the words: "By Bill Dennison." *Ahh!* he thought. *So that's a byline. Cool!*

He quickly started to read the article and then started reading all the other articles on the front page, hoping to find his. What was written under his "byline" didn't seem very familiar. He thought his story must be misplaced. Had Mr. Avery made a mistake? All this story was about was Uncle Bob's long and hard work to fulfill his dream of building a sailboat. The article contained dimensions, descriptions, and a brief history of what it took to build a sailboat in your basement. But there was no mention of not being able to get it out of the basement. No remark about the necessity to dig out his basement wall. There wasn't even a word about Uncle Bob's attempt to hide this mistake from public notice.

Billy didn't understand. What happened to *his* story!

He walked into the smoky *Union* office and stood in front of Howard Avery's desk. Ash fell from his lips as he turned. He had an envelope in his hand with Billy's name on it. Inside was a check for five dollars.

"Nice story, ace," he said. "See ya." And with that he turned back to his old Royal.

"But what about the story I turned in?" Billy asked, puzzled, and moving quickly toward anger. "You took all the juicy stuff out! What happened to the goods I uncovered?"

"You mean the big scoop, ace?" Avery asked with something like disappointment on his face. "Here's the big scoop, kiddo. The big scoop is that you don't embarrass people just so you get your name in the paper. You don't expose mistakes just because they happen. And you don't humiliate your family. Good reporting takes bravery, but it also takes a little common decency. That's the big scoop, ace."

Billy hesitated, confused, not knowing quite what to do. He couldn't think of anything to say, so he simply walked out and got on his bike, figuring that his career as an *Onion* reporter was finished. By the time he rode halfway home, he had moved from confusion to embarrassment from what Mr. Avery had said.

As he pushed through the back door, his mother was in the kitchen fixing supper. "Billy," she said, "where have you been?"

He wasn't sure what to say. He didn't want to tell her about his little talk with Mr. Avery, but he really didn't want to lie either. He said, "I don't want to talk about it, Mom."

"I read your article in the *Union*," she said with pride in her voice. "You kept that a big secret. I didn't know that you were doing that."

"I didn't really do that," Billy said.

"What do you mean? It has your name on it."

"I mean I didn't write what Mr. Avery printed. He rewrote what I did and that's what's in the paper." Billy felt the heat in his face and knew it was turning red. He was embarrassed to think what his mother might think of his stupid mistake in writing the article that he did.

"Tell me what happened," his mother pleaded.

He was reluctant at first, but then all his confusion, anger, and mostly embarrassment rushed out. "I don't want anyone to know I couldn't write an article that Mr. Avery would publish. Please don't tell Dad. And for sure, don't tell my brother. He'd never let me hear the end of it."

His mother grabbed his arm and was patting his back when she asked, "You don't like the feeling of being embarrassed?"

"Of course not," he said. "Who wants to be embarrassed?"

"Not you ... not Uncle Bob."

Billy never wrote for Mr. Avery again, but he didn't stop writing, and most importantly, he never forgot the truly big scoops he uncovered that day: that simple decency trumps success and to always think about how what you write feels to the person you're writing about.

That's the big scoop!

A Sweet-and-Sour Thanksgiving

On the southern shores of the Katamacasi River, thirty-five miles from its destination at Lake Michigan, nestled in the rolling woodlands of a very rural county, was a small town called Potowasso.

It was late in the evening the night before Thanksgiving. Two inches of snow had fallen and refreshed the tree lines and hillsides with that unmarked purity of early winter. The temperature was holding at about twenty-eight degrees, but it was the nervous preparations that warmed the households in Potowasso. That's what warmed Bobby DeGlopper's home that night.

Bobby's mother was in the kitchen humming as she rolled dough for pies—one pumpkin, one custard, and one she called "Dutch cherry." Bobby's dad was in the dining room with old, yellowed sheet music and some ancient slips of paper containing scribbled words and some chord notations that he used in conjunction with his worn Washburn guitar. He tuned the scratched-up relic, making painful faces as he struggled to find an elusive pitch. Bobby halfheartedly watched the snowy television reception and fussed with the vertical hold, trying to get Perry Como to sit still. Bobby's sister, Cathy, played with her toy dishes and an upside-down corrugated box she used as a stove, which their dad had to cut a flap in the front so that she could use it as an oven. Cathy had cut out a picture of a turkey from a *Look* magazine advertisement and slipped it on a small pan into her pretend oven.

"How hot should I set the oven, Bobby?" she asked.

"Huh?" Bobby grunted, paying her little attention.

"The turkey! How hot?"

"I don't know," Bobby said. "Maybe about a thousand degrees to make sure it kills your germs!"

"Mommy! Bobby is saying I have germs!"

His mother's response was lost on Bobby, as his attention was captured by his father strumming the chords to "Over the River and through the Woods." A frighteningly dark realization struck Bobby and knocked the wind out of him. Mom was cooking and Dad was not. Dad was playing his guitar when he normally would have been beside Mom in the kitchen. This was such an alarming insight that Bobby ignored the chance to pull his sister's pigtail as she got close to him and jabbed her "germy" fingers in his face.

Dad wasn't helping in the kitchen. Dad was the "turkey guy." Therefore, turkey wasn't being made in the DeGloppers' household, and that meant it was the dreaded year that everyone went to Aunt Corrine's and Uncle Jacob's for Thanksgiving dinner, akin to an unwanted trip to the dentist.

"Dad!" Bobby squawked. "You're not making the turkey!"

"No," Bobby's dad answered easily. "This is the year we go to—" But before he could finish his sentence, the high E-string on his guitar snapped. It served as an omen of holiday woes.

His father's face showed the same kind of pain that he felt, the equivalent of fingernails on a blackboard—Thanksgiving at Corrine's. Dinner at Aunt Corrine's was always a trial, and his dad knew it as well as he did.

"We go to your aunt's house today," his father said, nearly in a monotone. "And it will be fine." He was not convincing Bobby of either that fact or his sincerity. Then they looked at each other with what Bobby thought was a mystical, father–son mind meld, in which through unspoken gestures they were accepting their uncontrollable, jointly dreaded fate.

Bobby's mom read the silence accurately and quickly tried to inject a positive spin on the doom he and his father were feeling. "We're going to Aunt Corrine's. And I don't want to hear a single word of complaint out of either of you!" She gave the sharpest expression of warning at Bobby's father, of which he was grateful.

It was just a year ago that the family had suffered the first in a couple of strained family gatherings. A year ago, Aunt Corrine had set a new low for the DeGlopper Thanksgiving ritual. She was invited to have it again, out of family rotation, as an attempt to let her regain the self-respect she had lost by serving a steaming platter of Swiss steak—not turkey, but Swiss steak!

Bobby remembered and blurted out, "No *turkey?*" And the silent reaction of the rest of the family by this vocalized astonishment confirmed the solidarity of everyone with young Bobby. And he recalled the painful expressions as they all stared at the tomato-lathered chunks of beef that renounced all hope for stuffing.

Aunt Corrine was a very sensitive person and had not grown the necessary emotional callus to a family that could be very open and honest. Everyone felt bad about their candor that sent Corrine from the room, looking as if she was about to cry and saying, "I never do anything right!"

Though a sad day for the DeGlopper family, it was a boon for Gleeder's Market, which sold a number of turkeys at nonsale prices the next day. It also served to greatly compromise Aunt Corrine's tenuous status in the clan from odd duck to eccentric. But it wasn't until that Labor Day that she achieved full alien status.

The alienation came by way of music, not menu. Music was one of those elements that held the family together. Steeped in the heritage of harmony, the Degloppers and the VandeVelders had merged in Bobby's mother and father's marriage. Never had two families been so in tune with the love of music, coupled with a generous endowment of talent.

Mac—Bobby's father—could strum, pluck, and cajole a guitar into making more music than most folks could get out of their stereos and a dozen Time Life music collections. And Mac's melodious tenor voice made women swoon and men cry. Evelyn, Bobby's mother, was a fine soprano and substituted on the piano and organ at First Church of Potowasso. Rumor had it that giving increased by 30 percent when she stood in for Glenda Glowers, the regular keyboard musician. Grandma VandeVelder loved to sing, and songs loved her back. Grandpa played his harmonica with such flair and dexterity that people figured he must have two tongues in his mouth and a third lung in his chest. Bobby's Aunt Trina, his mom's sister, was as good a singer as her sibling and simply a magician with her banjo. Her husband, Bert, had a bass voice that rumbled agreeably in the very bottom of human register to the point of making tuba players jealous. Uncle Jacob, the oldest brother of Trina and Bobby's mom, alternated between his rich baritone voice and the honey that he enticed from his slide trombone, while all the time his feet were tapping rhythm like Gene Krupa's hands. And the slew of kids and grandkids joined in and were vocally somewhere between the Osmonds and the Vienna Boys' Choir. Well, that's how the DeGloppers and VandeVelders heard everyone anyway.

Aunt Corrine became a DeGlopper by marriage to Bobby's uncle, Jacob. Everyone had been so glad to have Uncle Jacob and his great voice back in the family gatherings. He had moved away because of business and now had moved back into the area as a regional sales manager with the Purina livestock feed division. As good as Jacob's voice filled out the harmony, Aunt Corrine's voice was a distraction.

Bobby had heard her say how much she loved music. And whenever he was near her when the family was singing, he knew she had a remarkably strong voice for such a small lady. Bobby's father once said, when he didn't know his son was listening, "If singing was a vocal ballet, Corrine was stomping around in army boots." Another time he had said, "Proper pitch is as elusive to that woman as rain in Death Valley."

Bobby's family loved to sing and make music together and found their identity in blending their gifts. Corrine was like the anti-musician. And this fact demanded a great measure of restraint for a family so used to hearing heaven in their mingled voices and instruments. Aunt Corrine's presence had made their musical paradise into the glee club from Gehenna.

Bobby had a feeling that it was just a matter of time before Aunt Corrine's torturous tones would finally break their resolve to ignore it. To Bobby, it was like Chinese water torture over a span of years—soon the victims would break.

Stories from Potowasso

When the family sat on the back porch of Aunt Trina and Uncle Bert's cottage on Labor Day afternoon and Corrine attempted a high F in "The Good Old Summertime," Uncle Bert snapped. The unbearable pain that had been intensifying with each and every family sing-along finally poked through, and like a dog stuck with a porcupine quill, Bert howled in pain. "Holy smokes, Corrine, don't crucify it! Oh, man, you sound like a banshee being tortured, a sick coyote caught in a trap, like a church treasurer hearing about the pastor's raise. Could you hold it down to a shriek!"

And there it was, out in front of God and everybody—the truth about Corrine's voice. Was it possible she didn't know how bad it was? If Corrine had any suspicion of talent, it was pretty well down the crapper after that. Everyone was pretty shocked at Bert's outburst, and it caused a great stillness in that belabored holiday.

Aunt Corrine was vocally silent the rest of the day, though her soured face was loud enough. No amount of coaxing could pry another note out of her. Finally, the music that was a trademark of these reunions ended like a train run out of tracks.

The interlude between Labor Day and this Thanksgiving had been a natural break in get-togethers, and no one was creating a reason. They didn't talk about how the next holiday would go; they pretty much just lived in denial—another talent they were endowed with. Bobby wondered what would happen the next time the family got together. Would they sing or not? It was hard to believe such a long and important part of get-togethers would be forgotten. Then the next logical question was that if they did resume their family music-making, would it be any fun? Would it ever be the same?

They never talked about it, so Bobby figured the family was just going to ignore it, like it never happened. And if they could get through this one holiday with no music, the issue would disappear. Bobby also concluded that his elder DeGloppers and VandeVelders must have all believed as children that if you closed your eyes the monster under the bed couldn't see you and, therefore, couldn't get you. So Thanksgiving was going to be like a long night with eyes closed against the monster of last Labor Day. The sun would again come up and the hobgoblin of holiday past would vanish—another problem solved by hiding from it. Everyone just had to keep the subject from coming up, and they could live through one holiday without making music together. It wouldn't be fun—or honest—but it seemed the wisest and easiest way past the problem.

So, as the whole family gathered for this Thanksgiving for the second year in a row at Aunt Corrine's, everyone seemed resolved to be cordial and musically mute. Maybe it would work. Maybe group denial would succeed.

As folks began to arrive, each was met at the door with Aunt Corrine's welcome, which consisted of a curt "Hello" followed by "don't fret, we're having *tuurrkeeey!*" This was accompanied by a delightful caustic grimace. Bobby guessed that the concept of being thankful was being reserved for ending this day.

The turkey was dry, but it was turkey. The stuffing was scarce, the mashed potatoes were lumpy, and the gravy was thin. Someone had brought that orange Jell-O and then ruined it, Bobby thought, by adding shredded carrots. He wondered about putting broccoli in the pie. Aunt Corrine made everyone—children included—take a dab of cranberry sauce. Everyone hated it, but to skip this tradition was tantamount to breaking a commandment, and the family complied. Maybe it was like accepting penance for past sins. And so a mediocre but traditional meal was consumed and discomfort set in, just like it was supposed to.

They remained at the table after the meal and the dishes were cleared and before pie was served. It was the common practice of the DeGlopper–VandeVelder clan to recite a chronicle of the "things we're thankful for." The kids usually began with teddy bears, bicycles, desserts, best friends, and gerbils. Then they worked their way up to Grandma and Grandpa.

The adults had a more difficult time. Usually you could count on a litany of musical motifs, followed by family and food as the prevailing topics of gratitude. But this year, with memories of a Thanksgiving of Swiss steak and the Labor Day debacle, there were new dimensions and, therefore, the need for a more creative list.

Bobby's dad was appreciative of his employment, which the group approved of heartily. Aunt Trina was thankful for a safe year. This too was agreed with, but not a very satisfying bid.

Uncle Jacob tiptoed around the food issue by offering an acknowledgment of something he dubbed "God's bounty." The adults seemed to understand, but Bobby thought it was either an old ship or something to do with wolf pelts.

Bobby's mother decided to go philosophical and offered "peace" as a possibility. Grandpa VandeVelder picked up on the safety of such themes and went right to theology. "Grace!" he uttered, as if he was trying to convince us more than simply to list it.

"Yes!" Uncle Bert enthusiastically endorsed the idea. "God loves us because he loves us, not because of what we do!"

"Unconditional love!" Aunt Trina said, as if a correction.

"Not because of works of righteousness, but by the unmerited gift of salvation!" Uncle Bert's deep voice thundered, and the whole group seemed to move back in their seats, apprehensive about a possible fist slamming on the table and perhaps an offering plate passed.

"I thought Grace was a girl's name," little cousin Amy squeaked.

"No, stupid," her brother, Andrew, began but was abruptly cut off by his mother's stern eyes.

As Bobby listened to the debate, he remembered his catechism lessons and Pastor Quark's emphasis on this very principle: "Grace is an unmerited gift." With that in mind, he said, "Grace just means we're accepted because we're God's children."

"What do you mean 'accepted'?" his brother asked with more than a trace of ridicule.

"I mean," Bobby answered, "it's not about being good enough, but about being given a gift. It's like your birthday. You get presents even if you broke Mom's favorite teacup the day before."

His brother was ready to make fun of him some, but Bobby's parents and the rest of the adults were quiet and almost seemed to be staring at the little theologian with a mixture of astonishment and respect. In fact, Bobby was certain that pride was creeping onto his dad's face.

It seemed to Bobby that with his words, he had crossed into the realm of being an adult. He had said something serious, and at least the grown-ups were taking it that way. Then, like an adult thinker, he thought some more and made another clever insight. He had come up with one more illustration of grace for the group to chew on. He said, "It's like God inviting you to sing in the choir without a tryout. Even if you can't carry a tune, he thinks you sing great!" And he looked at Aunt Corrine and smiled.

Uncle Jacob's eyes became the size of saucers, and Grandpa choked on his water. Bobby's mother moved her mouth but was unable to form words. His dad shut his eyes so tight Bobby thought they might come out his ears. Uncle Bert began swallowing hard, and each gulp seemed to trigger a new shade of red on his face.

How could a conversation that had climbed to such spiritual ecstasy plummet to such temporal misery so quickly? The kids were confused, but Bobby was sure that all the grown-ups knew he was using their musical evaluation last Labor Day as an example of not using grace, as they were all sucking air, like they had been punched by a huge common fist.

That's when Aunt Corrine stifled a little snicker and then erupted into a colossal bellow of laughter. Puzzled, yet relieved by her behavior, the adults, one by one, started chuckling, which was more contagious than yawning and more comforting than even Grandma's chocolate fudge. Chuckles became gales of laughter. Relief rushed out with abandon and tears ran. Smiles spread and table and knee pounding commenced.

After a few minutes they began to compose themselves, and that's when Corrine said, "I never understood God's grace so well." She looked at Bobby and asked, "Do you think God would even let me into his choir?"

"No sweat," Bobby replied. "God would probably ask you to sing a solo!"

They burst into another fit of laughter, which mushroomed when Bobby added, "He'd probably even love your Swiss steak too!"

With a smile as warm as Corrine had ever shown, she said, "I'm just thankful God loves turkeys ..." she paused to look around the table and then added, "and bad singers!"

The family, including Aunt Corrine, sang songs into the night and every holiday gathering after that. The out-of-tune pitches she added to every number seemed to complete it, not deplete it. And each note she sang became a reminder of God's grace, and how the family received forgiveness for each and every sour note they sang in the very long song of life.

Hunting Season

Deer season in Potowasso is a lot like Halloween, which it follows. It is loaded with tricks and with treats. November 15 brings with it treats for King Dixon. It means a rush of activity at his hardware and sports shop.

King opens early the week before the season and stays late every night. He's like a quartermaster for a huge militia that just got word of a major action. He's a gunnery sergeant giving instructions to infantrymen and women on how to maximize their success. Old campaigners and raw recruits alike come for provisions and munitions. It's an endless column of pick-ups and recreational vehicles moving toward the front lines. King Dixon sets up extra registers and will make extra deposits for about three weeks running. Yes indeed, King Dixon finds lots of treats about this time of year.

But, just down the street, the tricks are being pulled. As busy as King's Hardware is, it's that slow down at First Church in Potowasso. Pastor Quark is psyching up for another small crowd, made even smaller by the fact that opening day falls on Sunday. Quark is working on his text from I Timothy, hurrying so that he has time to make up the bulletins. The rush is on account of his secretary, Clara, who has taken the big week off, as usual, to head north for the hunt with her husband, Tom. Tom plows snow for the church … except during "the season."

Pastor Quark was reading a commentary, exerting great effort to keep his mind in first-century Ephesus and the young preacher Timothy. He was gripping the book like it was the only thing keeping him from falling from some great height. His mind drifted, nonetheless, to the empty pews and the dismal singing that was certain to describe the coming Sunday service, decimated by all the hunting absences. His self-righteousness indignation swelled like a balloon ready to burst. He started to see every precious word from the text, as written explicitly for backsliding hunters, and heretical sportsmen. He worked up such resentment that he was on the verge of letting loose with one loud and profane—"darn it!" But he settled for a whispered "gee-whiz!" as good pastors are prone to do, and he feebly attempted to pound his desk.

Clarence VanHuizen, deacon and sage, walked in on Pastor Quark as he was rubbing his hand and wincing. "Ya hurt yourself, Pastor?"

"No. Yes. Not really. Kind of."

"Thought maybe you cut yourself on that two-edged sword."

The tall gangly minister squinted through his over-sized, dark-rimmed spectacles. "Huh?" he squeaked.

"The Bible," VanHuizen explained. "It was a joke."

"Oh, yes," Quark said, with a pitiful forced chuckle. "I get it now. Yes, 'cut myself.' Very good."

"Somethin' got you bothered, Pastor?" the older man asked.

"Hmmm?" Quark queried.

"You seem distracted."

"Oh," Quark said, measuring what he wanted to express. "I'm just thinking about the low attendance during deer season. It's like people show up until they find something better to do. And I really don't see the attraction." He spoke while shaking his head slightly. "Cold, wet, sitting and waiting for some poor animal to mistakenly walk too close to an opportunist with a gun."

"You ever been hunting?" VanHuizen asked.

"I don't think so." Quark pursed his lips and rolled his eyes, trying to find some forgotten memory of hunting but could find none. "No. Not hunting. I went fishing a couple of times though," he said with pride. "Caught a big Sun-gill!"

"A what?" VanHuizen asked. "You mean a bluegill, or do you mean a sunfish?"

"They're not the same thing?"

The deacon just shook his head, trying hard not to laugh at this pathetic city boy. Then an idea sobered him. An idea that was as logical as it was alarming. Before he thought it out much he asked, "Why don't you try it? Hunting that is. Come with me and a couple of guys out to my cabin. Get a feel for it. Experience what we experience."

"Oh, my," Quark said, looking as uncomfortable as someone trying bungee jumping for the first time. "I don't think I could. I mean there's this office work I have to do. There's the service on Sunday." The thin minister was groping for excuses as if for his life. And then with triumphant jubilation, he struck upon the perfect justification. "I have no hunting gear. Not even a gun. Thanks anyway."

"Well, I can let you borrow one of my guns, and I might have an extra jacket you could wear. And you don't have to miss church; you can come back for the service and then return for the rest of the day."

"I probably won't have my sermon done on time, but thanks."

"Take it with you. Work in the cabin. Saturday we'll be out checking our favorite spots. You can have all the peace and quiet you need."

"Maybe you don't have the room, or the others don't want me intruding on their turf?" Quark was getting desperate for excuses. "Or maybe the other guys will feel—you know—uncomfortable around—my presence might be—don't they like to use colorful language and talk about things that maybe having a preacher around would inhibit them?"

"Oh, horse hockey!" VanHuizen said, with a look of hurt. "We aren't totally depraved, ya know." Then VanHuizen went for the jugular. Quark may have been a man of the cloth, but he was a *man* of the cloth. "But, if you don't think you could handle it …"

Pastor Quark was quiet for a moment, while color rose in his cheeks. Thoughts and images raced through his stodgy mind. Then an idea struck him. If he did it, he could say he had tried it, and find a whole new inventory of reasons to be offended by this strange tradition. Maybe even uncover some evil practice that he had never known about.

So with the resolve of a missionary hearing the call to a far off savage land, "I'll do it! Yes, I'll go, if you promise I can be back for Sunday service."

"Done," VanHuizen said enthusiastically, but Quark detected some hesitation and regret.

That night, Quark broke the news to his wife. She looked at him through supper as if some stranger had taken over her husband's body. Thinking of him as a hunter must have been extremely difficult. *One of the boys? A redneck with a collar? A hunter with a halo?* None of these monikers would be easily applied by the one who knew him best.

The next day, the self-satisfaction of facing the lion in his den filled Quark with reflections of heroic proportion. The man of God, walking into the enemy's camp, wielding his weapon of choice—his Revised Standard Version—fending off their clever arguments and overpowering their reasoning with sharp blows from Paul and a couple of upper-cuts from Jeremiah.

Then another picture flashed in his head—three large antlered bucks gutted and hanging from a makeshift pole ... next to one scrawny dangling minister. This image cooled his missionary zeal, and in this nippy atmosphere Quark began the pursuit of a kinder and gentler type of instruction for those misguided sportsmen. He would prove to be just one of the guys, and they would be surprised at their false notions about men with soft hands and large glasses, mistaken about men of the cloth—they would see his was flannel.

This new strategy conjured up visions of sorrowful, repentant apostates falling over themselves seeking his forgiveness for such erroneous misconceptions. And then Quark was inspired to an even greater vision, spurred on by a more remarkable apparition: Grown men with three-day beards and tears running down their cheeks, as they looked in awe at the massive buck—big as a Clydesdale, with a rack like a leafless maple tree—dwarfing their meager deer, so small in comparison that theirs would seem to be of a different and lesser species.

Quark could hear chants of "You're the best hunter we've ever seen!" and "Please, teach us your ways, O great one!"

Quark came back to earth with a disturbing idea, one that seemed contrary to his grand notions. If he was to be one of the guys, he had to have what real guys have. A real guy doesn't borrow a gun or hunting jacket. No, a real guy has his own. It would be hard to appear their equal, if not their better, while borrowing equipment. Quark entered King's hardware, ill equipped to sustain any equilibrium in the midst of such temptation, that a hunter puts himself in annually. The good reverend had no experience to help control the urges that hunters are up against year after year. There were perfect barrels and beautiful carved wood stocks of guns that have never been fired. He caught sight of exquisite boots by Sorel and Red Wing that promised such comfort and warmth on the coldest of days. Quark glimpsed gloves and mittens of rare materials that vowed to protect the digits and keep them limber. He tried on some caps and hats and other exotic headgear with flaps and straps and snaps. He browsed the variety of undergarments that would aid in maintaining body heat.

Then he explored the rack of jackets, coats, parkas, and whole suits of flame-orange. He felt like a kid when the J.C. Penny's Christmas catalogue arrived. The near inebriation that can overwhelm even the most experienced hunter, nearly locked the preacher into the grip of that annual illness—*u-gotta-havit-itis*. But a glance at the price tag hanging on a Weatherby rifle sobered him quickly. Yet he was only sobered, not defeated. He would just have to choose carefully, and with thrift in mind.

He settled on a used Mossberg that King insisted was "like new." Quark picked out a sensible hat, warm but relatively inexpensive, mittens with a finger flap, some thermal long-johns, the boots that advertised "leather-like" vinyl. And then he paused at the wide range of outerwear. He decided that a one-piece insulated jumpsuit would be the most economical. But they were still very expensive, and as he looked them over, he was mentally reviewing his latest credit card statement. Having his charge denied after all this shopping was almost too horrifying to contemplate. Then he saw the sight that warmed the cockles of his heart—a red tag that proclaimed—"Irregular: Reduced for Clearance!"

He pulled the gaudy orange, zip-up insulated snowmobile kind-of-suit out of the rack and held it up. He noticed that though he was holding it above his head, the elastic cuffs nearly dragged on the floor. He checked the size—it said "small."

"It's an irregular," King said from the next aisle, noticing the preacher's focus. "It says small, but it's more like a XXL tall. It'll be real comfortable for sitting," he assured Quark.

"Is that the only irregular part of it? The size?" Quark asked.

"Well ... there may be a couple of unusual stitches and maybe the sleeves and legs are not perfectly proportioned. But it'll do the job."

Now Quark could see that one leg hung a little lower than the other, and the collar seemed to have been sewn on a little crooked. *But the price* ... the savings alone on this suit would pay for the gun that he would probably never use again, this time for that matter.

"Sold!" Quark said, with the definitiveness of a final "Amen!"

On Saturday afternoon, VanHuizen's Ford Explorer pulled into the parsonage driveway, and he tooted the horn. Quark emerged from the door looking a lot like an orange Zeppelin with glasses. His Mossberg was partially sticking out of a too short gun case, but a *real good price*. He was introduced to Butch and Junior DeGroot, who seemed nice enough, and very accepting of his presence on this expedition.

They drove out of town, down a dirt track, and eventually to the cabin. They unloaded the gear and supplies. The three other men, he was told, hit the woods scouting for signs and preparing tomorrow's hunt. Quark stayed at the cabin, needing to finish tomorrow's sermon. I Timothy was coming along quite nicely though. He sat at the table, shivering in his thin slacks and oxford shirt he had worn under his warm orange suit. He checked a dozen times to see if the door had cracked open, feeling a definite draft. He added more wood to the fire and sat closer, trying to forget the cold and concentrate on the sixth chapter of this epistle—a warning against false teachers.

Teach and urge these duties. If any one teaches otherwise and does not agree with the sound words of our Lord Jesus Christ and the teaching which accords with godliness.

Quark could not help but feel a little superior, a little bit more godly, as he pored over the sacred page while the others paraded through the woods, probably sneaking peppermint schnapps and spitting tobacco into the fresh fallen snow. They thought they were having fun, but what was fun compared to what he was doing—composing a word from God. A word that so many would not hear, because they would stay reveling in the forest instead of sitting still in church.

As he mixed the text with what he was feeling, he scratched the whole sermon and rewrote a new masterpiece, which could only come through divine revelation and with the speed of spiritual light. His new masterwork was a *magnum opus* about the frivolity of those who don't keep the Sabbath; the proud, stiff-necked generation of church-slackers. Hunting in lieu of church attendance was nothing short of prideful self-centeredness.

When his companions came back as it turned dark, Quark laughed to himself that these foolish idlers were unaware of how they were helping his insight into the corruption of hunting, and on their turf, composing what would most likely expose their pagan rituals, and end them. He was also amazed that they could hide their drunkenness and pretend to be so willing to fellowship and fake goodwill and civility. They could camouflage their proud, irreverent character, but Quark knew it was just underneath the surface. He was not fooled.

Taking inventory of these guys' outfits, and their old guns, he decided he was the best dressed and best equipped of them all. Inwardly he shook his head at their second-rate hunting gear. Dirty, worn, ripped coats, and guns with scratches and hints of wear on stocks. His first time hunting and he was outhunting the hunters. He went to bed snug and smug.

Quark woke in the middle of the night, freezing. The fire was out and the wind cut through the cabin, as if all the windows were covered only with screens. Shivering, he got out of bed long enough to slip into his insulated suit. A little cumbersome, but it was warm.

He woke suddenly with the rising sun blazing through the cabin window. He looked at the wind-up clock and saw it was much later than he had planned. He jumped out of bed, slipped his glasses on, grabbed his notes, and rushed out of the cabin as he went to lead the saints in worship and deliver his verbal blow on sportsmen like those he left sleeping.

It had snowed in the night and no plows had cleared any of the roadways, and so it took Quark longer then he had anticipated getting back to town. He wouldn't have time to stop by the house and shower and shave, so as he drove, he used the cordless shaver he had packed. He was glad that he had on a shirt and pants that would be appropriate, and he would put on the spare paisley tie he kept at the office, don his robe, and be presentable for worship.

The parking lot had quite a few cars in it for the opening day of the season. He parked in the space near the office entrance, grabbed his recreated sermon, and sprinted for the door. As Quark dropped his Bible and papers on the desk, he reached for the zipper on his bright orange jumpsuit. It was a large brass zipper, and it held its place as if it had been welded there. At first Quark was annoyed, but as he heard the organist begin the introit, panic began to rush through him. He gripped the zipper with more resolve, and pulled with all his might. He was now perspiring profusely, and his fingers hurt from the pull of this stuck and fixed zipper. And he looked at the little tag that said "Irregular."

A knock on his door, and a frantic voice trying to remain polite asked if he was ready.

"Yes," Quark answered. "I'll be right there."

He was now jumping up and down, trying to add leverage to his futile attempts to dislodge the stubborn zipper. Sweating and exhausted, he slumped in his chair, closed his eyes, and tried to conjure up an appropriate prayer—none seemed to meet this present need.

Quark was resilient, if nothing else. He would not be stopped by this orange opponent. He would simply put his robe on, over the heavy suit, and pull the legs up, and no one would be the wiser. And that is just what he did. Quark reached the pulpit door, just as the choir was finishing the call to worship. He opened the door and went directly to the pulpit.

From the pews, the people could hardly believe their eyes. Here was their pastor, but significantly different. They were shocked as they examined this strange sight. It was their pastor's familiar face, though glistening with perspiration, and his hair a bit mussed. But as their gaze worked its way down from his neck to his torso, they were taken aback. Their extremely thin pastor had apparently put on about a hundred pounds since they had last seen him. Shoulders high and wide, chest enormous, and even his arms appeared to be swollen. It was like someone had attached the minister's head to the body of the Michelin man.

As the service went on, Quark's glasses began to fog up, and one orange legging slipped down. He was nearly overcome with heat exhaustion and held on to the pulpit to maintain his footing. Taking a deep breath for confidence, he looked out on the flock as he absently flipped pages on the pulpit Bible. When he finally found I Timothy, the sixth chapter, and looked up to address the congregation, he spotted three unexpected congregants in the last pew—VanHuizen, Butch and Junior DeGroot. He took a double-take and found amused smiles on their faces. *Why had those irreligious hunters shown up?*

Then he saw what he hadn't seen in his preparation for the service—the people. He saw the pews that were filled, instead of those that were empty. He saw the folks who were present and stopped focusing on who was missing.

He looked down at the text, and his eyes read it before his mouth spoke it. And Reverend Quark's face began to turn the color of the hunting suit inflating his black robe. And then he did what he knew he must—he read the scripture for the day. But as he read it, he did so not so much to those who were sitting in pews, as to himself.

> Teach and urge these duties. If anyone teaches otherwise and does not agree with the sound words of our Lord Jesus Christ and the teaching which accords with godliness ... HE IS PUFFED UP WITH CONCEIT, he knows nothing ...

Quark, in his overstuffed robe, puffy arms, and inflated ego, closed the book, and found he didn't have near as much to say as he'd thought. Without a sermon, the hunters were able to get back out in the field sooner than they had thought.

Deer hunting went on as usual, but Pastor Quark vowed he would not. He made a concerted effort to stop hunting what was wrong and begin looking for what was good. And above all else, in his future sermons, be would always preach them to himself before he preached them to the congregation.

That year, Quark bagged a real trophy—one of many points that pricked his conscience and one with a lot of meat to chew on.

That's deer hunting in Potowasso.

Hill Folk, Flatlanders, and Table Settings

Up in the hills, northwest of Potowasso, lived a bevy of individuals who, to the less unique residents of town, seem a bit curious. They were located on the drive up Snake Road and turning onto Broken Wheel, which got its name from an old mill on the Muck River that broke once and became a convenient road sign. When you made that turn you slipped through some sort of time portal and ended up in the land of the hill folk. Though the hills were not large, they contained a mountain of differences from the town below. Architecture, which could be seen in pictorials from the magazine *Better Hovels and Vegetable Patches*, was modest and often leaning. It felt like Appalachia but sounded like the Upper Peninsula, where Latvian was a common language.

But these hill folks were known for being hospitable and trusting, where their cousins in other hills seemed to be unwelcoming and a closed society. One of the prominent families in the hills was the Grinblats. Maris Grinblat was the head of the clan, but Coriava certainty ruled her roost. Maris and Coriava had three sons—Yurky, Sairvy, and Janis, who went by Janny. Mostly they worked with their father in the woods, cutting trees for the nearby pulp mill and also cutting and delivering wood to those crazy people down below who would actually pay for something as common as firewood. Maris was fond of saying in response to this peculiarity, "Next thing you know, they be buyin' water from the grocer! Ha! Ha!"

The youngest Grinblat, Janny, was the educated boy who took to schoolwork and was the first of his family to go not just through the eighth grade but right on through high school. He was a handsome lad with a winsome personality. Janny was also the most social. He was the one who took the trailer of wood down to Potowasso and delivered cords of oak to the residents. He was also the boy who went with his mom, Coriava, to help with the shopping.

One day when he was with his mother, who was complaining about the poor selection of dried beans and expensively small portions that they were bagged in, Janny saw an angel. Her name was Anna VanderLoop. Janny knew her from high school but had never had much occasion to speak with her. He was surprised when Anna's mother called his name. "Janny? Janny Grinblat?"

"Yes, ma'am," Janny replied.

"My husband just bought a new wood stove and is interested in some firewood. He wants a delivery very soon." It didn't seem to be a question, but Janny took it as one.

"Yes, ma'am. I can bring a load tomorrow if that is okay?"

"That would be permissible. Come between one and two o'clock. And bring a broom to sweep up any mess you make on the driveway. We live on—"

"Oh, I know where you live." Janny interrupted her and turned red as he caught young Anna's eye.

To help save some time and cut to the chase, this encounter would lead to a fairy tale of a romance—the beautiful princess from town meets a serf from the hills. Finally, two years to the day after that conversation in the grocery store, they were engaged to be married. Janny's folks were delighted, and Anna's folks, especially her mother, were less delighted and more just conceding the fact. But they were basically good parents and ultimately sought only their daughter's happiness and did their best to convey their blessing to this unlikely pairing.

As Thanksgiving approached, the families had their first experience with the where-do-we-go-when-there-are-two-families-to-consider concept with in-laws. Mother VanderLoop made the decision simple: "You will come to our house for Thanksgiving dinner, Janny! Won't you?" It wasn't the words as much as the squint of her eyes and the contraction of tiny muscles in her jaw that enforced her "invitation."

Attempting a gracious gesture, while feeling constrained, Janny offered to provide the turkeys. "How many do you think you'll be needing, Mrs. VanderLoop?"

"It is not necessary," the matron answered. Then she added with curiosity, "And what do you mean 'how many'?"

"How many?" Janny quizzed. "I mean *how many*! How large a gathering is it going to be, ma'am?" Janny hadn't quite gotten the nerve to call her "mother" yet.

"There will be only eleven, counting yourself, Janis."

"Okay. Then you'll only need a couple of good-sized ones!"

Mrs. VanderLoop said, "I'm confused. Why on earth would you need more than one turkey?"

Janny was momentarily perplexed. Then it dawned on him. "You buy your turkeys from the grocer, don't you, ma'am?"

"Well, of course, where else—" But before she finished the question, the light broke over the situation. "Do you raise your own, Janny?"

"No, ma'am. We hunt 'em wild!"

Janny saw something like shock cross her face. What was she thinking? Maybe she had visions of some darkly mutant bird lying on a bed of parsley sprigs with a ragged hole the size of a fist running through both sides of an already-scrawny bird. Maybe she was envisioning her husband asking their guests, as he carved the bird, "Dark meat? Or would you like some *darker* meat?" He tried not to smile at the flatlander's possible aversion to wild meat.

He scoffed inside at Mrs. VanderLoop's apparent aversion to having turkey dinner, yet at the same time he was less than happy about the thought of having some store-bought bird. He could just envision a bleached-white mound of chemically enhanced meat that was called turkey, a mountain of rather bland, pallid protein between a mound of mashed starch and a quivering pile of gelatinized cow hoof called Jell-O. He wondered what kind of gravy came from those chemically obese birds. *Burned-flour gravy it must be.* It even crossed his mind that he might want to eat before he went to such an unappetizing meal.

"I've never tasted wild turkey," Anna said in wide-eyed innocence. "Could we have both?"

"That's not necessary," Mrs. VanderLoop said, looking for help or something from her husband. But Mr. VanderLoop just shook his head and fanned his hands as if to say, *Don't get me involved in this!*

"Why don't I have my mom fix one and I'll bring it as my contribution to the dinner," Janny said. "And you prepare what you are used to."

Mrs. VanderLoop, having lost the aid of her husband, turned to her daughter and began gesturing to Anna like a third-base coach giving the sign to a batter to lay down a bunt. No help there either.

"That's a great idea!" Anna said. "What do think, Mom?"

Seeing that Anna hadn't picked up the sign or was just ignoring the silent direction, Mrs. VanderLoop set her jaw, fixed her mind, and closed the discussion. "No. We will supply the turkey," she said stiffly. Then with some lines on her face relaxing and her voice calming fractionally, she said, "Thank you for your offer, Janis. But you will be our guest and need not bring a thing."

Janny reluctantly agreed, unfamiliar with accepting the hospitality of someone without bringing some sort of appreciative gesture. He resolved to let Mrs. VanderLoop do Thanksgiving her way and be happy with the fact that he was with the girl he loved and with her family members, who were very important to her.

Coriava Grinblat graciously supported her son's decision to go to Anna's for Thanksgiving. As much as she would have enjoyed their presence with them in the hills to celebrate the bounty they received from God in the carving of the traditional Thanksgiving turkeys, she knew that they had to share the kids they had in common. But Coriava had one request: for Anna to join the Grinblats in a Thanksgiving dinner on the following Sunday.

Anna and Janny began to realize some of the changes that their marriage would generate as they moved through the calendar, wrought with unforeseen conflicts. But they told each other that they were comfortable with this year's Thanksgiving dinner adjustment—

actual Thanksgiving with the VanderLoops, surrogate Thanksgiving with the Grinblats.

On the heels of that quandary came another: where to attend the official Thanksgiving church service.

The VanderLoops were members of First Church of Potowasso; the Grinblats belonged to St. Vincent Lutheran Church in Sweeney, a hill town about two miles away. Would they attend the predominately Dutch church or the Evangelical Latvian Lutherans? Both had 9:30 AM services on Thanksgiving morning. What would it be? Who would have the familiar hymns, who the unfamiliar ones? Who would have the comfort of the familiar? The VanderLoops and the loose formality and intellectual worship of the Dutch church, or would the Grinblats with the high liturgical and mysterious service of St. Vincent's? Both Janny and Anna discovered that they were both quite conflicted over this decision, more so than the dinner tradition, for sure.

Finally, Anna's clear head and amiable thinking blazed the trail of resolution. Because the VanderLoops were getting the real dinner day, it was only appropriate that the Grinblats get the worship service. It seemed logical and fair to everyone ... almost everyone. Mrs. VanderLoop gave her verbal approval, but the flexing of her facial muscles and cold look gave another message. Yet with this one reservation, the Lutherans would have one more attendee than usual. Janny was thankful for this concession but was still disappointed at missing his family's holiday dinner.

Sunday rolled around, and it was Anna's turn to experience someone else's traditions. After the cozy service at First Church of Potowasso, Anna and Janny headed for his home. Everyone was involved in the crowded kitchen preparations—even Anna. Then they gathered at the table for the holiday meal.

The long wooden table that had never been covered in all the years that he could remember was strewn with a sharply pressed white tablecloth. The plates didn't match, but three of varying sizes were stacked upon one another at each place setting. Coriava had put two forks and two spoons at each place. There were tumblers—

polka-dot, plastic, and glass ones from some old laundry detergent promotion—at each place with water and an ice cube in each. When the food was served, it was in all sorts of bowls and vessels that Janny had never seen. And his mother only brought one wild turkey out at a time on a platter that looked an awful lot like the piece that his dad sorted nuts and bolts on in his garage.

It was time to be seated at the table and begin the feast. Janny's father sat down at the head of the table and opened the big family Bible that usually just sat on the coffee table in the front room. But today Mr. Grinblat read a lengthy psalm and gave an even lengthier prayer. The Grinblat boys ribbed each other and laughed through the meal. They had pie in the living room, while Janny and his family screamed at the television and the bad calls by the referee.

It was a wonderful day for Janny, and as he took Anna home that evening, she told him what a nice time she had had.

As they pulled into the VanderLoop driveway, Anna said, "Though it was different from what I am used to, I had fun and love your family."

"Yeah, they're great!" Janny said but also thought, *What's not to like about them, and what's not to love about our traditions?*

Thanksgiving morning began traditionally for Janny as he walked into church with his family. The only difference was that Anna was with him. They found their usual seats about two-thirds of the way to the front of the beautiful and ornate sanctuary. Later he learned from Anna that she was surprised to see the kneeling benches and amazed at the intricacies of the bulletin that she perused. She told him that the sanctuary was darker and more mystifying than First Potowasso, and it smelled of some bitter, yet not unpleasant, incense that smoldered from that hanging brass thing that she had never seen. She mentioned the beautiful candles and cross that sat radiantly upon the altar table. And she realized that they were clearly the focus of the sanctuary. The music, she commented, was slower and composed of more minor keys than she was used to, yet it helped promote that sense of mystery that she felt when she first entered

St. Vincent's. All in all it was a lovely and moving service, but she confessed it was not what she was used to.

After church, it was time for Janny to experience the new and unfamiliar. They drove to the VanderLoops' home and soon went to the formal dining room and sat down for the Thanksgiving dinner. Janny was a bit dazed by the table setting, unsettled by the dinnerware overwhelming the huge table by mere quantity and set in such immaculate symmetry. He wasn't sure he dared move a piece. There was beautiful white china with two gold rings circling the outer rims, surrounded by silverware that was really *silver* and not stainless steel, as he was used to. Every serving dish, each salt and pepper shaker, cups and saucers, butter plates, salad bowls, dinner plates, and whatever all the other smaller plates stacked upon the big plates were called—all matched. Janny had never seen all the dinner plates match at his house, and usually the serving dishes strangely resembled the pots and pans that the foods were cooked in.

Janny found his name embossed on a little seating card on a tiny silver tripod at one place. He supposed that it marked the place he was to sit, and not just a prop for some new ice-breaker game. *How pretentious,* he thought. At least it put him next to Anna.

As they sat, Anna's father made a rather elaborate event out of reading a psalm and then offered a lengthy prayer with enough "thees," "thous," and "O-O-O-O Loooords!" to fill an eighteenth-century revival sermon.

When the prayer was complete and the order to serve and eat was given, Janny was hesitant. *What on earth do you do with all these forks and spoons?* he thought. There were cups and saucers next to etched glass goblets for water. Everyone else seemed so comfortable with the extra paraphernalia and all the accessories that seemed so foreign to him. How he missed his home and family traditions right now.

He was nearly ready to break the fast by reaching for the turkey platter, even if it was the most sterile and antiseptic meat he had ever seen at such a feast, when the kitchen door swung open and a Hispanic girl came in with what must have been a maid's outfit. In she came, carrying a giant turret of soup and started ladling it out. *Soup is a meal in itself,* Janny thought. But he would bravely endure this and many other traditions of his soon-to-be-bride and her family.

Finally, the meal concluded, and none too soon. Janny had never spent such a long and agonizing time at a dinner table. He could not remember if the food tasted good or not, because the pressure to eat it correctly, with the right utensil and from the suitable plate, seemed to obscure all taste. For Janny, it was a bit like what the church service seemed to Anna, who had related her experience on the way home after her adventure at St. Vincent's.

Janny did his best to give Mrs. VanderLoop compliments on the splendid dinner but wondered if he shouldn't tell the nice girl who served it the same. She had likely actually done the work. But Mrs. VanderLoop was ready to accept all praise and never attempted, it seemed to Janny, to deflect any of it.

The rest of the day was a mixture of good posture and the appropriate nodding of the head as Mr. or Mrs. VanderLoop regaled the family with bizarre experiences at the "club" or at the "theater" when they were in "the city." Janny was intrigued that people got together and discussed bridge strategy and who was the best soprano today.

No one cheered as the Lions got their first score or even when they won the game. It was received like facts from a life insurance actuary. It was different, but it was their day and their way.

Finally, the holiday at Anna's ended, and none too soon for Janny. He jumped in his cold car and headed for home. He passed the front lawns with blow-up pilgrims and the Swattleberg farm and its worn but colorful turkey painted on a large sheet of plywood propped up by the front porch. As he approached his own driveway, he was assured of sanity by the lawn without decorations, just a warm glow from the kitchen window revealing steam from a toasty room, where his mother was probably preparing leftovers for a late snack. This small country home was a wonderful place to live and go through the seasons and celebrate the big days as well as the common ones. He was a very lucky guy.

Walking toward the back door, he put his hands in his pocket to ward off the chilly night air. His fingers discovered something that he couldn't identify. He pulled it out to find a little seating card with his name embossed on it. Anna must have stuck it in his coat pocket after the dinner at her home. *Silly girl.*

He walked into the mudroom outside the kitchen, sloughed off his shoes, hung his coat on a hook, and knocked on the glass-windowed door before he turned the knob and entered. "Hi, Mom," he said.

"Hi honey," she answered back. "How was your day? How was your dinner?"

"It was fine," he said automatically. "Smells good here."

"You're not hungry, are you?"

Janny shrugged and smiled sheepishly.

Then his mother noticed the card in his hand. "What's that, Janny?"

He brought it up to his face and looked at it, almost surprised, forgetting he had it. "Oh this," he said, shaking his head. "Just a memento from the pretentious VanderLoop Thanksgiving extravaganza."

"Let me see," his mother said and took it from his fingers.

"Mom, you wouldn't believe all the hoopla that goes into a holiday at that house. More plates and silverware than I could count, a maid serving soup before the real meal, and this pretentious placard on the table so the stupid 'hill kid' wouldn't sit at the wrong place!"

She examined the card and then looked at her son.

"What I wouldn't have given to be here with you guys today. I mean, it was brutal."

"What is wrong with this nice card?" she asked, looking back at the embossed table marker. "I think it's nice."

"Mom," Janny said, "it's just a big show with a lot of fanfare to cover up the shallow traditions they have. I'd rather be with my own family. Here we don't need place cards!"

"But why do you like it here? What is better here than at the VanderLoops?

"Well, everything: the food, the atmosphere, the company, and the plain, down-to-earth table setting."

"Was the food terrible?" Janny's mother asked.

"No. It was pretty good. But it was different."

"Were they nasty? I mean, was it an atmosphere of hostility, or did they openly belittle you?"

"Well, no! Of course not."

"They didn't read the Bible and pray before the meal?"

"No, they did that."

Then, raising the little table card up, she asked, "Did they tell you they put this out so you wouldn't sit in the wrong, stupid place?"

"Well, no, Mom! It's just the symbol of their rich, pretentious ways."

"Really," she said. "It seems like you had food, you weren't ridiculed, and they showed reverence. What was so different there than here?"

"Well," Janny began but couldn't figure out what to add. Then, as if inspiration had struck, he said, "Here I feel at home! Here I know I belong!"

His mother smiled with what looked to Janny like pity. Then she handed the embossed card back to her son and said, "This looks just like what you say you like here."

"What do you mean?" Janny asked, perplexed.

"I mean a place card is just that: a card that says 'you have a place.' Instead of seeing all the differences, why didn't you see this match? They weren't showing off their rich ways; they were letting you know that you had a place at the table. Their table is now your table. You're the rich one, my dear. You now belong at two tables, in two homes, and with two families. Now that's something to really be thankful for!"